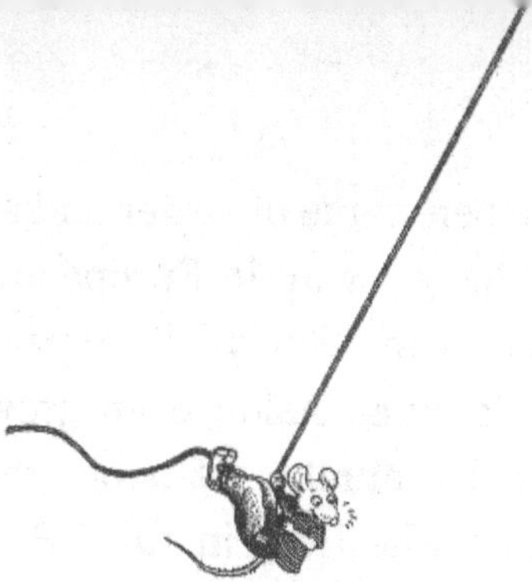

MOUSE ATTACK

THE AMAZING ADVENTURES OF ARVEE THE MOUSE

'Magnolia' is the pen-name of writer and artist Manjula Padmanabhan. She grew up in Europe and South East Asia. Her comic strip, 'Sukiyaki', appears weekly in *Business Line*, Chennai. Aside from grown-up books, she has published a number of books for children as author–illustrator. She lives in the US with no cats, plants or children.

Other books by Magnolia

MOUSE INVADERS
The Exciting Escapades of Arvee the Mouse

MOUSE ATTACK

THE AMAZING ADVENTURES OF ARVEE THE MOUSE

written and illustrated by

MAGNOLIA

hachette INDIA

First published in 2003 in hardback by Macmillan Children's Books
First published in paperback in 2004 by Macmillan Children's Books
A division of Macmillan Publishers Ltd
20 New Wharf Road
London N1 9RR Basingstoke and Oxford
Associated companies throughout the world
www.panmacmillan.com

First published in India in 2019 by Hachette India
(Registered name: Hachette Book Publishing India Pvt. Ltd)
An Hachette UK company
www.hachetteindia.com

SRD

ISBN 978-93-88322-31-7

Hachette Book Publishing India Pvt. Ltd
4th & 5th Floors, Corporate Centre
Plot No. 94, Sector 44, Gurugram - 122003, India

Typeset in Georgia 11/15.8 by
by Manmohan Kumar, Delhi

Printed and bound in India
by Manipal Technologies Limited, Manipal

FSC www.fsc.org MIX Paper from responsible sources FSC™ C043100

CONTENTS

Prologue: An Awful Shock 1

1. Beyond the Table's Edge 6
2. Contact! 13
3. The Drainpipe Home 17
4. Invasion of the Rats 24
5. Painful Memories 30
6. Dangerous Differences 36
7. An Intruder 42
8. Midnight Message 48
9. CAT-astrophe! 55
10. No Sleep for Arvee 60
11. Fight or Flight? 68
12. Antastic! 73

13. Battle Plans 81
14. Journey to the Unknown 88
15. Relief – and Horror 94
16. Pasha's People 102
17. Escape! 110
18. A Thrilling Ride 118
19. The Cracker Caper 125
20. An Explosive Idea 134
21. Lizard-back Riders 141
22. Swept Away 146
23. Look Out! 152
24. The Roach Approach 159
25. A New Start 170

Acknowledgements 177

PROLOGUE: AN AWFUL SHOCK!

Arvee threw on his dressing gown and tidied his whiskers before hurrying to the door of his study. 'It's only seven o'clock!' he thought crossly. 'Hardly the time for visitors!'

Nevertheless, he was a polite mouse and when someone knocked, he was bound to acknowledge that fact. Even if it did disturb his early morning meditation. He stepped out – and got a nasty surprise.

Not just one visitor, but several Outsiders!

There were never any strangers in the Laboratory. It was strictly off limits. His own Dr Shah was always saying how specialized this Laboratory was and how the humans who were allowed access to it were specially screened . . .

And there was Dr Shah. He was talking to the strangers, three of them. They were paying close attention to what he was saying. One of them seemed rather short for a human. Arvee assumed that this was a child. He had never seen a real child, only pictures, in books.

He wondered why Dr Shah had summoned him. He walked warily up to the edge of the table on which his private quarters were placed. He was quite tall for a white mouse, all of ten centimetres, and very fit. His large pink eyes twinkled like rubies and his whiskers formed a handsome, silvery halo around his aristocratic nose.

As he neared the edge, he heard Dr Shah explaining, 'He hates being disturbed this early, so he may not come out – '

Arvee cleared his throat diplomatically.

Dr Shah turned and caught sight of him.

'Ah – there you are!' he said. He smiled broadly, but Arvee sensed he was embarrassed. 'Arvee,' said Dr Shah, 'I want you to meet . . . your new family!'

No wonder he was embarrassed.

Arvee, a scholarly mouse with a list of degrees to his name, was being evicted from his laboratory home to live as that most helpless of beings – a house pet!

The next few hours were some of the most harrowing of Arvee's entire life. His personal belongings were packed up, while he stood by, powerless. No one consulted him, no one asked his permission. A decision had been taken, which would turn his life inside out, and that was that!

When Dr Shah came out to the car to bid a last farewell, Arvee was at his most formal. 'Goodbye, Dr Shah,' he said, 'it's been a pleasure knowing you.' Then he turned and vanished into his travel case without a backward glance.

The past erased. The future? A blank slate.

The journey lasted a long, long time. All the way, Arvee sat staring out of his travel case which, fortunately, had been placed facing the rear window of the car. He refused to pay attention to his new 'family', though he could hear their conversation. By listening carefully, he gleaned what he could about his situation.

In the car were a father, a mother and a little girl of around ten. Her name was Mohini, though Arvee didn't know that till some time later. Her parents called her Mo. She sat with her nose practically inside Arvee's travel case. Her warm, milk-scented breath filled the air around him, but he refused to acknowledge her. He knew she couldn't see him from where she sat. He was too upset to care.

Apparently, Mo and her parents had been planning to make this trip for some time. Dr Shah had spoken to them about Arvee months ago.

Bringing him home was something that Mo had been looking forward to for many weeks. When she wasn't breathing into his travel case, she was bouncing up and down on the back seat of the car. 'What does he eat?' Arvee could hear her ask her parents or, 'What does he do in the evenings?' or, 'Will the doll's house be good enough for him?'

'Doll's house!' muttered Arvee to himself, outraged. 'What does she think I am, a toy?'

But there was nothing he could do about what she or anyone else thought. He had never been out of the Laboratory before, so he had no experience of life Outside. Neither had any of his colleagues. Everyone he knew had only ever lived in the Laboratory.

In the Lab there was Order, there was Routine. Meals were served punctually. During the day there was the Library and the Computer Room. In the evenings there was the Maze to walk around in. And at night Arvee had a small, but charming, Zen garden all to himself, where he could rake the gravel in contemplative patterns. Or he could collect the flask of hot chocolate made for him and take it up to bed where he could drink it while reading a mystery novel.

Would all or any of these familiar assets be available in his new home? If not, to whom would he complain? Worst of all, would anyone in the new residence be able to speak to him? Few humans, even in the Lab, were capable of Advanced Communication.

The prospects so far were not promising.

Mo had been trying to say things to him. 'Oh please,' she had said, several times now, 'oh please, little mousey, please look around at me – please! Just once?'

Poor Arvee's heart sank to the bottom of his well-manicured toes.

'Oh no!' he thought. 'Baby talk!'

1

BEYOND THE TABLE'S EDGE

Some days later, Arvee was standing in the observatory of his new home looking around his estate. He had to admit he liked what he saw.

Spreading out on every side was the top of an immense, circular table. It was covered in green baize cloth, pinned tightly around the edge so that it looked like a beautifully smooth lawn. Dotted about the lawn were plastic trees. Beside some of the trees, park benches had been placed.

The glassed-in observatory was at the top of the three-storey doll's house, which stood at the centre of the estate. Arvee could not see the front door, but he knew that over the door was a sign framed in toothpicks, with the name *Mercara* hand-printed neatly upon it.

Aside from the observatory, the house had four bedrooms, a dining hall, a drawing room, and a cosy study filled with the books he had brought from the Lab. In another room, which he called the Music Room, there was a grand piano that really played. The walls were decorated with framed postage stamps from around the world. There was a kitchen and, just next to it, a sweet little breakfast nook.

There was an overhead tank filled with fresh water every day. The bathroom had a flush toilet and a bath as well as a shower. There was a pantry in which the stock of food was topped up every day by Mo herself. The armchairs were padded with real foam. Instead of a TV there was a slide-viewer with a light at the back, and many beautiful scenic sights for Arvee to contemplate.

Nevertheless, standing in his observatory, he sighed to himself.

What was the point of all this magnificence – there was no other word for it, it was magnificent – when there was no one to share it with?

Mo, for instance, was an exceptionally good human and Arvee was growing very fond of her. She really cared for Arvee's comfort and she talked to him whenever she had some time left over from school, from homework and from her parents. And though she couldn't understand him, her conversation was no longer baby talk.

All the same, she was human and very large and a child. Whereas Arvee was a mouse and very small and an adult. A scientist, at that. He needed someone who could not only understand what he said, but who shared his interests too. He needed friends to argue with or play chess against or discuss his ideas with. He needed companions.

But there weren't any.

Being a practical mouse, and one who was not used to accepting that sometimes there is no solution to a problem, he had set himself the task of finding ways to occupy his time.

Currently, his occupation was to make a detailed survey of the room in which his table stood. Using the binoculars, which had come with him from the Laboratory, he had taken to spending every morning mapping sections of the room, one small area at a time. Eventually he might write a brief paper titled 'The Human Habitat and What It Reveals About the Species'.

Starting with the north wall, working clockwise, he had so far encountered a vast, glass-fronted bookcase. It had taken him a week of careful observation and notes to clear three shelves. Today, he was about to start on the fourth and final one when . . . *What was that?*

A whisper of movement, right there, on the floor behind the shelf!

Hardly daring to breathe, Arvee focused the binoculars with care.

He could see the tiled floor, then the back corner of the bookcase where it met the floor. Once, twice, three times, Arvee raked the area with the binoculars, trying to see what had caused that flicker. But in vain.

He was about to give up, when a small object caught his eye.

It was so easy to overlook that he had mistaken it for a bit of fluff. But he looked again, concentrating hard. And there, sure enough, was the object.

It was a rubber sandal of the type that has blue straps and a white sole. It looked rather worn down and thin. And that was all. No sign of the owner, no indication of what sort of animal had worn it.

'Well!' said Arvee out loud to himself. 'What *can* this mean?'

There were two possible options. Either he could go down right away. Or he could watch from his house till the owner of the sandal came back to fetch it. 'After all,' he reasoned to himself, 'anyone whose sandal is so worn out probably can't afford to lose it.'

He clamped the binoculars on to a stand in the observatory so that they wouldn't shift. Then he settled down to watch, taking care not to shift his gaze for more than a few seconds at a time.

But, by late afternoon, there had been no change in the situation. The sandal remained where it was and the owner, if there was one around somewhere, had not appeared to claim it. Shadows were gathering in the room. Soon it would be too dark to see anything either way.

'Oh dear, oh dear,' worried Arvee. 'I'm going to miss my chance.'

Then it was night and there was nothing visible beyond the pool of light shed upon *Mercara* from a Japanese paper lantern hanging directly over the table.

The room in which the table stood was a small, square, in-between space with Mo's bedroom on one side and the bathroom on the other. It was used for storing things like old tennis shoes and out-of-use toys. Besides the glass-fronted bookcase against one wall, there was also a window, always shut, along the only other wall. Through the window, the lush, well-tended garden was visible.

At nine thirty, Mo came in to say goodnight. Then she turned out the Japanese lantern and the room was plunged in darkness. Arvee, of course, was free to turn on the lights in *Mercara*. His power supply came from batteries that Mo changed periodically.

Arvee helped himself to some cold potato salad and chips made of puff pastry. He was thinking about what he should do. He desperately wanted to know if the slipper was still where he had seen it. From the size of the slipper, it seemed very likely that the owner was a mouse. And, if so, he absolutely had to make contact!

At the same time, he knew he shouldn't get off the table. It was one of the things that Mo had asked him not to do. She had sounded very serious and even hinted that there was some danger involved. But he hadn't actually given her his word that he wouldn't.

'Oh!' he exclaimed out loud. 'Decisions are *so* difficult!'

In the end, curiosity won.

'I'll be very careful,' he told himself. 'I won't stay long. And I'll go right away, right now.'

If the slipper was still there he would hide himself and wait to see if someone came to retrieve it. If it was a mouse, then that mouse would be likely to wait until the overhead light was off in the room before venturing out to get the slipper. And perhaps that mouse would wait a short while before even trying. Mice were known to be cautious, after all.

Arvee told himself that he would wait by the slipper for an hour. If no one came within that time, he would leave a note requesting the owner to do likewise, suggesting a place and time for a more formal meeting.

Arvee walked across the tabletop, carrying his toolkit with him. All around the edge were the smooth, round heads of tacks that held the green baize stretched and fixed in place on the wood.

It was a moment's work, with just a bit of grunting and heaving, to lever up the head of one of the tacks with the crowbar. By repeating the manoeuvre on opposite sides of the tack, Arvee was able to raise it up just high enough to slide his arm under it and grab its stem.

The next move was simple. There was a skein of embroidery thread in one of the store cupboards in his house. He had brought this along with him. Attaching the free end of the thread to the tack, he tied a firm knot.

'Thank goodness I paid attention during that lecture on mountaineering!' he said to himself. 'You can never tell when something's going to come in useful.' He gave the improvised rope a sharp tug just to be sure it would hold him. Then, putting his whole weight on it, he leaned over the table's edge.

From the window a ray of moonlight had entered the room. It crossed the table and fell over the side to the floor, looking like an arrow of light. It seemed to be pointing straight towards the slipper.

Here goes nothing, thought Arvee. Holding tight to his rope, he took a backward leap. As he did so, it seemed to him that he was leaving behind not only the tabletop but the last traces of his earlier life, the safe and predictable life of the Lab with its routines and its seminars.

If only Dr Shah could see me now, thought Arvee, swinging jauntily on the frail embroidery rope, what *would* he think!

2

CONTACT!

How suddenly huge and towering everything seemed at floor level! The table, which from the top was a flat, green disc, was now a great, dark canopy held up by a huge central column of carved wood. The glass-fronted bookcase loomed impossibly high, its summit lost in the cavern of the ceiling. The rug on which the table stood had pile as dense, for Arvee, as a garden of unmown weeds is for us. And everywhere, night shadows lay thick and impenetrable, with only the band of moonlight gleaming on the floor like a highway made of polished silver.

Reaching the place where the rug ended, Arvee saw that if he moved along the bright stripe of the moonlight and then a little to the left of it, he would be directly at the place where he had seen the slipper.

His delicate, shell-pink ears outstretched to catch the slightest sound, his whiskers a-quiver, Arvee stepped on to the lighted path.

He heard a gasp. Then a small, gruff voice said, 'You see? It *is* white!' Then – silence.

That was too much for Arvee. Standing there in the moonbeam, his pure white fur gleaming so that he seemed to be in a halo of light, he called out, 'Who's there?'

Nothing.

'Helloo-ooo?' How plaintive his voice sounded to him!

From the direction in which he was headed, there came a kind of rustling. Arvee decided that he must dare all and move towards the sound. Instantly, there was a further rustling. Another voice, but softer this time, said, 'Look! It's . . . it's coming this way!'

Arvee didn't know what to do. 'Oh – please,' he called out. 'Don't go!' He scampered forward until he was at the end of the lighted strip. Peering into the darkness immediately beyond the margin of light, he called out, 'Who are you?'

Silence.

'Are you . . . mice?'

Silence.

'Look! I won't harm you.' Arvee held his paws out to show that they were empty. 'Please. Won't you come out?'

Arvee thought he could just about discern a shape, a shadow denser than the darkness around. It might be a mouse or . . . it might not. Anyway, it didn't seem bigger than him.

'My name is – ' Arvee began but, before he could continue, a voice called out to him. It sounded firm and male, but also strangely fearful.

'Never mind your name! Wh-what *are* you?'

Arvee felt his heart race with pleasure. 'Why, why – I'm a mouse, of course!' It seemed so funny to have to say that. 'Don't I look like one?'

'A *mouse?* But – but – you're all . . . *white.'*

'Well, of course!' said Arvee, thinking: So they're not mice. Why else would they make such a remark?

There was a sort of whispered consultation going on. Then the first voice said to the second one, 'If it's *sure* it's a mouse . . .'

And the second voice said, 'But – what mouse would dare to stand like that, in the middle of all that glare? It can't be one – oh, it can't!'

However, before Arvee could think of what to do next, the dark shadow darted forward, grabbed his wrist and tugged him out of the moonlight. The paw felt like a mouse's paw.

'First things first,' said the voice. 'If you're a mouse, get out of that awful spotlight and come *here.*' And 'here' was where the slipper had been.

'Now then!' said the voice. 'Explain yourself, sir!'

Arvee, the breath knocked out of him by his sudden flight, couldn't find the words to say anything at all. Standing nose-to-nose in front of him was a being he couldn't find any description for.

A black mouse!

Who had ever heard of such a thing?

3

THE DRAINPIPE HOME

Don't let's talk here, please!' said the second of the two voices, urgently. 'It's too dangerous.'

'You're right,' said First Voice. Turning to Arvee, he said, 'Follow me, it's not far . . .'

First Voice led him a short way along the wall to the lintel of the bathroom door. Just where the door met its frame, at the corner, the wood was worn away so that a slender mouse could fit through.

First Voice said, 'I'll go in, then you follow and do as I do. You have to wriggle sideways a bit and you'll . . .' He disappeared into the door frame before completing his sentence. From somewhere inside the wood came the words, '. . . find it's not so difficult.' Arvee didn't need to be told this since he was used to the Laboratory maze, but he was too polite to say so. He crawled into the little space, then moved towards the right, his whiskers guiding him. He slid easily over and across, coming out suddenly on to a slippery, smooth surface of glazed tiles.

'Careful,' said First Voice. 'They're a little tricky to walk on.'

Arvee stood up. The gleaming white tiles of the bathroom spread away on every side. 'Ooh!' he said, feeling overwhelmed. 'Is this where you live?'

'Not exactly,' said First Voice, 'but quick! We can't stay here long – Ellie?' He was obviously speaking to Second Voice who had, in the meantime, also crawled through. 'Everyone here? Good! Let's go. I think I hear You-Know-Who.' And he scampered on.

Arvee sprinted as fast as he could, thankful for his sneakers, which helped him not to skid. He could hear the sound of Ellie's sandals flip-flopping behind him. It must have been her sandal that I saw, thought Arvee, as he drew up to where First Voice had stopped, just by the tub.

'Here,' said First Voice. 'Stay close. This bit takes some practice.' Where the floor joined the wall at the side of the tub there was a large, round drain hole with a heavy, metal grille. The grille looked a little bit like those perforated ladles used for deep-frying.

Ellie joined them, saying, 'Just do as I do.' She seemed to have lost some of her fear of Arvee.

A small portion of the grille had been broken. First Voice said, 'Hurry! I think I hear him!'

Ellie slid neatly in through the space in the grille while Arvee watched, wondering all the while who You-Know-Who was. A rope ladder made from twine and matchsticks had been attached to the grille and suspended under it. Stepping on to this, Ellie looked back up at Arvee and said, 'Just climb down towards the side of the drain till your toes find a ledge.' So saying, she disappeared.

Without pausing to think too carefully about what he was doing, Arvee followed Ellie. He hung for a moment on the ladder and smelled the cold, damp sewer under him. Then he climbed down. Even before his toes had touched the side of the drain, he felt Ellie's paw reach for his, to help him in. A passage had been hollowed out of the wall.

Looking back, he saw that First Voice was already swinging down on the rope ladder. In another trice, he too was standing in the passage with Arvee, panting slightly. 'Just in time,' he said.

There came a soft, swishing sound. The faint light that filtered into the drain from the gleaming bathroom was suddenly obscured. The grille creaked, as if something heavy had stepped on to it. Something with rasping breath.

'Who's that?' said Arvee, curiously.

First Voice shuddered as he answered him, 'Alphonso, of course! I'd rather not talk about him just now, please, if you don't mind.' And with that he showed Arvee down the corridor to his home.

Six mice lived together beside the drain. The eldest was Oldmouse Stringer, but Gramps was what the others called him. He sat by himself in a corner, with a piece of soft leather wrapped round his shoulders. He looked away into the distance and never said a word.

First Voice's real name was Stringer. He was Gramps's son, wiry and energetic. His vest and loose cotton pants were threadbare but clean.

His wife, Ding, was a tired-looking mouse with a sweet smile. In her arms she held the baby of the family, crying weakly and not looking well at all. He was called Moon Bum because when he was born his tail was white. He was known as Moonie for short.

Ellie was Stringer and Ding's daughter. She was small in build, but something in the set of her ears told Arvee that she had spirit. Unlike the others, she was dressed gaily, with a couple of sparkling sequins in her hair. Her long skirt was made from a bit of glittering sari-border that twinkled in the dim light. She wore a pink cotton blouse and a twist of pale pink chiffon over it as a scarf.

Standing next to Ellie, but a little apart from her, was her cousin, Toon. He was a teenage mouse, wearing torn blue jeans and a T-shirt. His hair was in a ponytail and his whiskers stuck out in an untidy bush round his nose.

In the dim light of their home, Arvee saw that his new friends weren't black but brown. They lived very simply, in an irregular space scraped out of the brick and mortar of the building.

The kitchen was a curtained-off area between two bricks. A shelf made of matchboxes held food-stores. The drain was used as a toilet. For showers, the mice went up to Mo's bathroom, to stand under a dripping tap. On the opposite side from the entrance tunnel, another tunnel continued elsewhere.

Tiny niches in the brickwork held pistachio shells used as oil lamps. Dancing flames from these little lamps filled the room with a soft light. Hanging from the wall on nails and pins was assorted family gear: bits of string, used blades, beads, some shiny ribbons.

Above the central area hung a ping-pong ball. It had holes cut into it and a pistachio-shell lamp had been suspended inside it. In a few places on the walls, raised designs of flowers and pretty little insects had been made with window putty mixed with white chalk.

Stringer introduced his family, then said, 'And now you tell us *your* name.'

'Oh – uh,' said Arvee, who felt as if he'd forgotten how to talk, 'Arvee.'

Ellie cocked her head to the side and said, 'That's an unusual name.'

'It's not exactly a name,' said Arvee, 'it's my initials, you see: R.V.'

'Initials?' said Ellie. 'What does that mean, "initials"?'

'Ah, um,' said Arvee, momentarily at a loss. He had never met anyone who didn't know the meaning of a word like 'initials'. Why, *everyone* at the Lab had initials.

Not wanting to offend Ellie, but trying to answer the question all the same, he replied, 'Well . . . my full name is Roussel Venkateshan Two-Hundred-and-Thirty-Seven-Thousand-Four-Hundred-and-Fifty-Eight. . .

The others gaped at him with blank expressions.

'. . . but I'm always known as Arvee – you know, "R" from the name of my Ancestral Laboratory and "V" from the name of the Research Scientist who is responsible for my clan, followed by my serial number.'

He stopped. 'Why?' he said, finally. 'H-have I said something wrong?'

Stringer was stroking his whiskers, worriedly. 'Well, er, no, but I mean . . .' He paused as if composing his words with care. 'We're not used to having such a grand name visit our home.' Then he took a deep breath, as if deciding to change the subject for the time being, and turned to Ding. 'Let's eat, shall we? I'm famished after all the excitement.'

Arvee's protests that he had already had dinner fell on deaf ears. The four of them – Stringer, Ellie, Ding and Arvee – were soon sitting together on a mat spread under the ping-pong-ball light, munching on puffed rice dipped in a spicy curry. Moonie was lying quietly in a walnut-shell cot. Toon had vanished.

Arvee gave the others a quick summary of his life up to that point, ending with, '. . . and you must visit my house!'

There was a slight pause. Then Ellie said, 'Speaking of which, we should be thinking about getting you back.'

'That's true,' said Stringer, his voice immediately tensing up. 'We don't have much time.'

'Much time?' asked Arvee. 'Much time for what?'

Ellie and her father exchanged glances. 'It's . . . a long story,' said Stringer.

4

INVASION OF THE RATS

'The humans named this house "Paradise Villa",' began Stringer. 'At one time all of it belonged to my family. The humans came and went, but *we've* been around for generations.'

He sighed. 'Good times don't last forever, I suppose. Two years ago, our prosperity and happiness in Paradise Villa finally attracted the attention of the rat gangs in the neighbourhood . . .'

'Rat gangs?' interrupted Arvee. 'What does that mean, "rat gangs"?'

Stringer looked surprised. He couldn't imagine a mouse who didn't know about rat gangs!

Ellie tried to explain, 'Well . . . you know what rats are, surely?'

'Of course,' said Arvee, smiling. 'There were rats as well as mice in the Lab.'

Stringer snorted. 'White ones, like yourself?'

Arvee nodded innocently. All the rats he had ever met had been research scholars, intelligent and dignified.

Stringer said, 'In that case, perhaps, the rats you knew were so refined that they had no memory of their traditional role in the animal world?'

'And what's that?' asked Arvee.

'Why – crime, of course,' said Stringer. 'Rats are the criminals of the animal world. Drugs, terrorism, vandalism – you name it, the rats are into it. They trade in slaves and they rig races and they run protection rackets. They are the meanest, cruellest, most dangerous beasts in the whole animal kingdom.'

Arvee was sitting with his mouth open. He hardly knew some of the terms Stringer had used. 'But – but – ' he stammered, 'no animals can be *that* bad.'

'But *they* are,' said Stringer, so forcefully that it came out as the closest thing to a roar that a mouse can manage.

'Papa!' said Ellie, trying to calm her father, knowing the state he could get into when talking about rats. 'You shouldn't be so biased!'

'I'm sorry, Ellie, but you know my views.' Stringer's outburst had woken Moonie, who started to cry.

Stringer picked up the baby and began pacing back and forth, his whiskers twitching with emotion.

Ding said quietly, 'These last two years have been a big strain on Stringer . . .'

Ellie said, '. . . on all of us.' She looked over to where her grandfather sat, silent, in a world of his own. Her voice was firm but full of suppressed anger. 'You look at us today and you wouldn't believe how things used to be, how well we used to live!'

She took up the story where her father left off. 'We don't know how and when the rats began planning to take over Paradise Villa. The first we saw of them here was about two years ago.

'The head of our clan, at the time, was a great-aunt of mine. She was the senior-most mouse in Paradise Villa, but she wasn't good at being a leader. She was simple-minded and vain. So when the rats came to pay their first visit, she was impressed by their flashy ways and fancy talk.

'The rats told her that all they wanted was to use the front veranda of Paradise Villa as a clubhouse. They promised to behave themselves. No drinking, no gambling, nothing of the sort would be allowed, they told her. Only the most well-behaved creatures would be admitted as members.

'My poor, foolish great-aunt! The rats gave her sweets and perfumes and told her how beautiful she was – while all the time they were getting to know their way around the house, getting ready to take it over.

'They waited till the hot season, when humans go on their annual migration.

'I remember it so clearly! Some of us were sitting and chatting in the drawing room. All of a sudden, we heard a strange sound from the veranda clubhouse. Like a soft rumbling. . .' She shuddered. 'I'll never forget that sound for as long as I live. It was the sound of two hundred rats or more, armed, gathered outside and waiting for the signal to strike . . .'

The atmosphere in the room was charged with the terror of that time.

Ellie continued, 'It didn't take very long. They came in all together. Their leader was with them – the one they call the Rat Lord. My great-aunt came running out. Someone had told her what was happening but she refused to believe it. The Rat Lord laughed in her face. And the younger, rougher ones called her foolish names, and made fun of her airs and graces. Then they pushed her aside and went towards her apartments saying, "We'll start with Milady's chambers!"

'They ripped everything apart. They threw all the furniture and clothes out on to the lawn, they smashed all the cut glass and china. Other members of the gang were waiting outside. They made a huge bonfire to burn whatever they didn't plan to keep for themselves. Then they went through the whole house, room by room. There was nothing we could do. The humans had gone away, taking Alphonso with them – '

'Excuse me,' said Arvee, 'I'm sorry, but I think I don't understand something. This is the second time you've mentioned a person I haven't met before – Alphonso?'

Stringer looked at him strangely. Ellie said, faltering a bit, 'Well, he's – he's the cat. The humans keep him as a pet.'

'Oh?' said Arvee. 'Is there one in the house? I should certainly like to meet him! According to what I've read, felines are fascinating creatures, full of rare intelligence and – ' But he couldn't continue. The other mice were looking at him as if he were speaking in Grasshopper. 'I've never actually seen one, except in pictures,' said Arvee, feeling – for the first time – that he must be the dullest, most inexperienced animal on earth.

Ding said, very kindly, 'How lucky – never to have seen a cat.'

Ellie said, 'Well, it's hard to describe a live one if you've only seen pictures . . . it's not just that they're much bigger than us, it's also that they . . . well . . .' She shrugged, helplessly, because she guessed that what she was about to say might come as a shock for Arvee. 'The fact is, they hunt other animals for food. I – I mean, small animals like us.'

'And they betray their friends!' said Stringer suddenly. His whiskers trembled. 'What Ellie's not saying is that the house cat Alphonso was once *our* cat. He came to the house when he was just a kitten. He wasn't like other cats. He was a pacifist, a vegetarian – the humans brought him up that way. He was absolutely tame and friendly. Until . . . the rats came.' Stringer looked away, too upset to continue.

'They bribed him with food,' said Ellie. 'His weakness is that he loves to eat. The humans didn't give him more than was good for him, but the rats . . . ! They fed him meat. . .'

'And he's never been the same since,' finished Ding. A silence descended upon the little group. Arvee found there were so many things to think about, so many questions, that he had nothing at all to say.

Just then he noticed a movement near the ceiling. Looking up, he saw an ant hurrying along. Almost at once, he realized it was just one of many ants, some moving in one direction, others going the opposite way. Occasionally, when two ants met, both stopped to twiddle their antennae, before bustling onward again. Arvee was so surprised to see them that he exclaimed out loud, 'Look – ants!'

Ellie giggled. 'They've been there all the time, silly! That's the ant line! They're everywhere, didn't you know? They're our news network.'

Stringer also looked up at the ants. 'Which reminds me – Arvee, it's time you went back to your home.' Arvee noticed now that one of the ants was carrying something white in its mouth.

'That's how we tell the time in Paradise Villa,' said Stringer. 'The ants carry different coloured flags for each hour. That white flag tells us it's one o'clock: Alphonso's off duty! Time to go!'

5

PAINFUL MEMORIES

There was no opportunity to talk on the way back to *Mercara*. Arvee, Stringer and Ellie were soon standing at the foot of the round table. The embroidery-thread rope was still dangling where Arvee had left it.

He turned to bid Stringer and Ellie goodnight. 'We'll have to work out a simpler system for you to come and go from my table,' he said. 'Then you must all come up for a visit.'

Stringer's nose twitched in the way of an anxious mouse wanting to get away fast. 'OK. And now – goodnight.' He held the rope steady as Arvee started his ascent, and waited till Arvee had reached the tabletop. Then he and Ellie vanished soundlessly.

Alone once more, Arvee wound up his makeshift ladder, feeling very thoughtful. 'I've learned a great deal tonight,' he said to himself. 'To think I've lived all these years and never realized that some mice are brown!'

Or that cats are dangerous house pets. Or that rats are known to have criminal tendencies. Or about the ant line and its uses. What new wonders awaited him in the morning? What new fears?

Two days later, scanning the entrance hole to the bathroom with his binoculars, Arvee saw the flash of a sequin lying in the dust. This had been agreed upon as the signal to ask him to come down from his table that night.

While waiting to hear from the Stringers, Arvee had used his time well. With his toolkit, he had carved a neat hole right through the floor of his drawing room and then through the strong wood of the tabletop. It was quite a job. When it was finished, he pushed a bottle cap into it, then covered it with a small velvet rug.

The hole would allow him to come and go from the table using the carved central table-leg as a staircase. And for the Stringer family to come back up too, he thought. He was keen to have his friends visit and stay with him sometimes.

But when he proposed this plan to them later that night, they looked uncomfortable.

All the mice were sitting once more in the central room of the Stringers' home. Toon was there too, improvising on a flute he'd made from a hard plastic straw. They had been talking happily enough, but when Arvee brought up the subject of a visit, a silence fell. He had to ask what the matter was before Stringer spoke up.

'You don't understand, Arvee,' he said. 'Your human friend won't be happy at all to see us with you. Humans don't like mice . . .'

Arvee wanted very badly to point out that *he* was a mouse too and that Mo definitely liked *him*. But Ellie spoke before he could say anything. 'Humans who see us behave really strangely. They run about, shouting – '

'They're afraid of us,' said Toon suddenly, putting down his flute.

'Afraid? Humans?' said Ellie, half laughing. 'You're crazy! How can they possibly be afraid of something as small as us?'

'I'm telling you, that's what it is,' insisted Toon. 'Humans think we'll run up their legs and bite their bottoms. They're *terrified* of being bitten by us! They think we have poison in our teeth. They think that if one of us bites them, they'll die . . .'

'And how come you know so much about humans all of a sudden?' said Stringer, a sharp edge to his voice.

Arvee looked at him in surprise. There didn't seem enough reason for him to speak harshly.

Now Toon was standing up. There was a defiant expression on his face. 'From talking to the Ratland Mice, as I'm sure you've – '

But before he could finish his sentence Stringer had leaped up and given the young mouse a smart rap on the end of his nose. 'I thought I told you never to meet those mice,' he hissed, his eyes blazing. 'They're scum! Do you hear me? Scum!'

Toon didn't say a word. Instead, he grabbed his flute and fled down the tunnel at the back of the small room.

Shocked by this sudden unpleasantness, Arvee tried changing the subject. 'Where does that passage lead?' he asked.

Stringer sat down again. The expression on his face was utterly weary and exhausted, as if he hadn't slept for weeks. 'Oh, nowhere, really,' he said. 'A little further, there's a chink in the brickwork. If you sit close to it, you can see out, just a tiny crack of a view. And you can breathe some fresh air. Toon sits there for hours with his flute.' Stringer sighed. 'I don't know what to do with the boy.'

In the soft light from the shell-lamps in the walls, premature white hairs in Stringer's fur glinted.

'What's the problem?' said Arvee.

'Just his generation,' said Stringer shortly.

'No, it's more than that,' said Ding.

Ellie said, 'It's the Ratland Mice. They're corrupting him with their gadgets and their lifestyle.'

'Hang on,' said Arvee. 'Who *are* these mice?'

There was a strained silence. Finally Ellie said, 'You see, when they raided Paradise Villa the rats didn't just throw us out: they gave us an option. . .

'The option of being their slaves,' Stringer said, bitterly, 'their servants.'

'You mean, you're not the only mice left in Paradise Villa?' asked Arvee.

Stringer said, 'Unfortunately, no.'

'*Papa*!' Ellie retorted. 'How can you say that?'

Stringer shook his head wearily. 'Ellie, you haven't been that side, you haven't seen what I've seen.' He looked up at Arvee. 'There were only two choices. Either we could live in this drain-side tenement, all of us. Or we could work for the rats. In their homes. Or in the bar. Or in the casino. Or . . . worse.'

He gave a low moan and slumped over with his head in his front paws. 'My own people! Working for the rats!'

Ding murmured, 'Why must we dump all our problems on Arvee's head? Let's talk of something else.'

At that Ellie jumped up and said, trying to be cheerful, 'That's true! How rude we've been! Tell us – tell us something about *your* life now.'

But Arvee had been quite affected by the thought of how much his new-found friends had suffered in the recent past. 'I'm sure we'll have time to talk about those things some other day. But for now I think there's something much more important to discuss.'

'What's that?' said Ellie, looking at him with her big, bright eyes.

'It's something I've been thinking about ever since I met all of you. I've not been able to get it out of my head. It's obvious that you have all been through a terrible experience. And so . . .' He gazed at the faces of his friends. Aside from Gramps who was in his own world, each one was looking at him with a slightly different expression. Ding was fearful, Stringer was uncertain and Ellie was curious. But he had their attention all right. 'The question is,' said Arvee, 'what shall we do to fight back?'

6

DANGEROUS DIFFERENCES

'Fight back?' sighed Stringer. His shoulders slumped. 'Wake up, Arvee! We don't have the resources. It's ridiculous to even think of it.' He shook his head and looked away.

'Not at all,' said Arvee. 'If we put our heads together, we can work something out.'

Stringer's nose twitched in irritation. 'Work *what* out? What can five little mice do against a battalion of well-fed rats?'

'But you said there are other mice – in Ratland,' reasoned Arvee. 'If we can be in touch with those mice, we could rally together against the rats.'

Stringer's nose twitched again. 'Oh, you just don't understand, Arvee . . .'

But Ellie sat forward. 'Well, it's better than doing nothing . . .'

'We could start a campaign,' said Arvee, 'to raise the awareness of all the animals in the house! We could hold demonstrations – '

'A campaign?' said Stringer, interrupting. 'And what sort of campaign, may I ask?'

'The usual kind,' said Arvee. 'Printed in magazines and newspapers, and of course on posters, banners, leaflets . . .'

'Posters? Leaflets? What're you talking about?' said Stringer. 'What are those things?'

Arvee didn't know what to say. It was like the time he had spoken about his initials and the others had not understood what he meant. 'Why, they're, umm . . . like *messages,*' he said, finally, 'written up on bits of paper and stuck on walls or handed out, so that everyone can read them and get to know about things.'

'Written, did you say?' said Stringer. '*Written*?'

The scorn in his voice was like a clenched fist. 'How does anything *written* concern us animals? We don't *read*!'

Arvee felt as if the floor beneath him had turned into thin air. 'Don't read?' he said, falteringly. 'Not. . . *at all*?'

Ellie was shaking her head, looking terribly sheepish. In the privacy of his mind, though, Arvee wondered for whom she was embarrassed. Was it for herself and her family? Or for him and his ignorance of their ways?

Stringer, however, wasn't looking shamefaced at all. His expression was serious. 'Listen, Arvee,' he said, there are many things you don't understand about us animals – '

Ding, who had been listening quietly all the while with Moonie asleep in her lap, said, in her soft way, 'Arvee's an animal too, dear.'

But Stringer snapped back at her, 'Not in some important ways! Not in the ways that make it possible for us to . . .' he chose the word carefully '. . . communicate properly, it seems!'

'Oh, Stringer!' cried Arvee, feeling pained and shocked. 'Of *course* I'm an animal – I've just had professional training, that's all.'

'But that's everything!' said Stringer, standing up. His whiskers were bristling slightly. 'Don't you see? Your famous professional training makes you different. *Too* different. That's what you don't understand.' Stringer turned to his wife and daughter. 'Do you remember that first time we saw him? We thought he was a ghost?' He turned back towards Arvee. 'We were frightened of you, with your white fur and your funny red eyes. Moving about in your fine house up there, you looked more like some kind of very special toy – a clockwork mouse with white fur and fancy clothes.

'And then, that night, when you came down, you were swaggering about in the middle of that strip of moonlight! Why – no mouse, no small animal in its right mind, would *ever* walk out in the open in that foolhardy way – '

'Papa, please!' said Ellie. 'Please don't be rude to Arvee!'

'I'm sorry, Ellie,' said Stringer, firmly. 'I have to speak my mind.' His expression was bleak, but he forced himself to continue. 'From the moment I saw you, Arvee, I felt uneasy about you. I felt you couldn't ever fit in with us mice – '

'But I'm a mouse too!' said Arvee, his voice coming out in a little wail. 'And I *am* an animal – just like you! I have feelings . . . I have thoughts . . . I need friends and company – just like you.'

'None the less,' said Stringer coldly, 'in many other ways, you're *not* like us –'

'*Papa,*' said Ellie, her eyes starting to fill with tears. She had an idea of what was coming.

'. . . and I don't think there's anything to be gained from being friendly with us!' finished Stringer.

'J-just because I'm different?' cried Arvee. 'Just because my fur is white? And – and – because I can read?'

'Arvee,' said Stringer slowly, 'what you don't understand is that amongst us *normal animals*, being different often means the *same thing* as being an enemy! And though I like you – I really do – I can also understand why we animals, we normal animals, have this rule.'

'Oh Papa, don't say that, please – don't do that to Arvee,' pleaded Ellie. She got to her feet too. 'Arvee isn't different in the ways that really count.'

'Oh, really?' said Stringer. 'Well, look: he's never dealt with a cat; he doesn't know why the rats are to be hated and feared; he's talking about written campaigns, about challenging the rats . . . and yet he knows next to nothing about the Rat Lord! He doesn't know what or who he's up against, yet he's all ready to start a "revolution". For all his education and his knowledge, he's never heard of our kind of problems before. He doesn't have the least idea of how impossible it is to solve them. And that's dangerous. Before he knows it, Arvee could get us into even more trouble than we're already in.'

Arvee waited for Stringer to finish, then he smoothed back his whiskers. 'Give me time, Stringer,' he said, 'to learn your ways! Teach me what I need to know and we'll pool our resources – '

'In the world in which I live,' interrupted Stringer, 'it's hard enough living inside a damp, dark hole above the bathroom drain, struggling to find food to keep everyone alive. We don't have the luxury to plan revolts. We don't dare to dream of a better tomorrow in case we lose even the little we have today. So I'm sorry, Arvee, but I – '

'Oh, please, Papa, please,' cried Ellie.

'I think it would be best for all of us if we didn't continue to meet.'

Stringer could look very stern at times, and this was one of those times. His ears were folded back, and his whiskers lay perfectly stiff and flat against his nose. 'It's very sad but, if you're ready, I'll escort you back to your house. Ellie . . . ?' He turned to tell her that she was not to accompany them.

But she didn't want to hear any more. With a stifled sob, she fled from the room, straight down the dark passage at the rear.

7

AN iNTRUDER

Back at the foot of Arvee's table, Stringer bade him a formal farewell. 'You probably don't believe me, but I'm really sorry about this,' he said, his voice sounding gruff. 'Maybe if things had been different . . .'

Arvee tried not to let his feelings show. With the shadow of a smile he said, 'I don't agree with your point of view, Stringer, but I like you too much to argue with you. And I'll never stop hoping that you'll have a change of heart.' He glanced up towards the top of the table. 'You know where to find me and I know where to look for a message from you. I really hope we'll meet again.' He would have liked to add a special word of farewell to Ellie, but he suspected that Stringer wouldn't be happy to know that Arvee had already developed a special fondness for her.

Stringer nodded in a businesslike manner, then turned and melted into the darkness. Arvee climbed up the central column of the table, feeling sad. It's all so pointless, he thought to himself. Why can't we just share all our differences and get the best of both worlds? Why does 'different' have to mean the same thing as 'wrong'?

He dragged himself up and through the hole he had made in his drawing-room floor, feeling heartsick. He pushed the bottle cap into place and laid the velvet carpet over it, thinking about all that had been said that evening, especially about the rats. Arvee had never heard of animals behaving so badly. Humans, perhaps, but never animals. In his experience, animals were nasty only when they were hurt, or frightened.

A big tear suddenly trickled down the end of Arvee's nose and splashed on to his sneakers. He recalled Stringer's tone as he had described the colour of Arvee's eyes. *Funny red,* he had called them. He had almost wrinkled his nose, as if the mere colour were something to feel disgusted about! 'Oh, *why* does it matter what colour my eyes are?' Arvee said out loud. '*Why* can't he see that we're all just animals together?'

And from behind him, a voice asked, 'Are you talking about Stringer-Uncle?'

Arvee's whiskers nearly fell out! 'Who – who's that?'

'Only me – Toon,' said Toon, stepping out from behind the shadow of the bookcase. 'Hi, Arvee . . . sir?'

'Toon?' gasped Arvee. 'Don't bother with "sir", just "Arvee is fine – but my goodness! What a shock you gave me! How *did* you get in here?'

'The same way you did,' said Toon. 'Up the centre of the table. You told Stringer-Uncle about it, remember?'

'But how did you leave the drain-house? I didn't see you going past us,' said Arvee, bewildered. 'Is there another exit?'

'Of course. From the back passage and out to the garden. Stringer-Uncle's really crazy to think that I spend the whole day sitting still with my nose stuck to a crack in the wall.'

'You mean he doesn't know about it?'

'He doesn't want to know. He doesn't want to take the least little chance of doing anything to attract the rats' attention – it's like he said, he's totally scared of losing even the little he has.'

Arvee started to nod and then he exclaimed, 'Hey! Wait a minute! You weren't there when we were talking about all that.'

Toon grinned. 'Electronics!' He held up a small item that had been strapped to his belt. 'I have a microphone hidden inside the ping-pong-ball light. In case something terrible happens, at least we'll know about it right away and can rush over, to help. It's just over the place where everyone usually sits to talk, right? And here's the receiver,' he said, as he snapped it back on to his belt. Even at a distance Arvee recognized that it was a fancy gadget, the very latest in Japanese microtechnology.

'Hmm!' said Arvee. 'That's come from your Ratland friends, I take it?'

'Yup,' said Toon, shortly. Then he added, 'You mustn't believe everything my uncle says about them.'

All this while, the two of them had remained standing in the drawing room. Suddenly, Arvee felt a twinge of hunger. He realized it was quite a while since he'd had his dinner. Time for a snack.

He said as much to Toon and, in a short while, both mice were sitting in Arvee's cosy little study, eating sandwiches and sipping hot chocolate. Toon was more comfortable sitting on the floor with his legs crossed, leaning back against the sofa. Arvee sat in his easy chair at the desk.

'It's like this,' said Toon. 'Stringer-Uncle says that the Ratland Mice are all slaves of the rats – but that's not true. There *is* a resistance movement. There *are* mice who would like to overthrow the rats.'

'But why don't you tell him all this?'

'He was too proud to work for the rats when they came,' said Toon. 'And now he's too scared to get involved with the revolt – he doesn't even want to know about it. He's lost hope, given up.'

'But how about Ellie?' asked Arvee. 'What does she think?'

'Cousin Ellie's really nice,' said Toon. 'I've always wanted to get her involved, but she's too protected.

Stringer-Uncle doesn't let her poke one whisker out of the house. He wants her to spend her whole life completely underground – and she's too nicely brought-up to fight him.'

'Er, well, OK, we can get back to that some other time,' said Arvee, unwilling to gossip about Ellie behind her back. 'Tell me more about your Ratland friends.'

'I'd like to do more than just tell you,' said Toon, 'I'd like you to meet them – they're not like my uncle. That's why I came to see you: to ask for help in organizing our movement, help with ideas and technical know-how . . .'

'Well!' said Arvee, his eyebrows shooting up. 'This is a quick turnaround of events. One minute I'm being shown the door and the next I'm being asked to join a revolution!' He shrugged good-naturedly. 'And how would I meet your friends?'

'That's the problem,' said Toon wistfully. 'It's so difficult to move in and out of Ratland. There are checkpoints and police and spies everywhere.'

'How many of you are there?' asked Arvee.

'About twenty.'

'That doesn't sound like much.'

Toon shrugged. 'No, but we have a lot of support from the other mice. They help us by getting us food or equipment – like this radio, for instance,' he patted the receiver on his belt. 'Or by placing our microphones in the right places so that we can listen in to the Rat Lord's important discussions.'

'I don't understand,' said Arvee. 'From where do your friends get the money to buy such things? They're usually quite expensive.'

'They don't *buy* them!' said Toon, looking a bit shamefaced. 'Whatever we get is either stolen from the rats or put together from the things they throw away or . . . or . . . whatever.'

'I can see,' said Arvee drily, 'why you can't explain any of this to Stringer.'

Toon shook his head ruefully. 'He'd really freak out! He's a stickler for rules and regulations.'

So am I, thought Arvee, but I want to believe that you're doing the wrong things for the right reasons. Out loud, he said, 'So how does your group move about in Ratland?'

'We have false identity cards,' said Toon. He reached into his pocket. 'Here! This one's mine – we got it made just a day ago.' It displayed his paw prints and a picture of himself wearing a white uniform. 'We mice can't move around Ratland without cards like that.'

Arvee examined it. 'Does this mean,' he said, carefully, 'that you're planning to leave the Stringers and live in Ratland?'

Toon was silent as he put away the card. 'I don't know, Arvee,' he said finally. 'My friends tell me that I must decide one way or another.' He had a faraway look. 'It's not easy, living in Ratland.' Then he looked back at Arvee. 'But it's not easy living with Stringer-Uncle either!'

8

MIDNIGHT MESSAGE

Toon thanked Arvee for the snack and left. He promised to remain in touch. But a day passed, then two, then three, with no word from him. No word from the Stringer family either.

Arvee felt lonely and sad. Every day, sometimes two or three times a day, he looked through his binoculars for the sequin down by the door to the bathroom. There was never the least sign of it. He began to feel that all he had seen and heard in the little house by the drain had been a sort of dream.

In the afternoons, Mo came to talk to him when she returned from school. Sometimes she would take Arvee out with her and sit on the steps that led from the veranda in front of her bedroom into the garden. Those were the only occasions when Arvee was almost happy enough to forget about the Stringers. The experience of feeling grainy, gritty earth underpaw, with the wonderful scents and sounds and sights of nature surrounding him, was something he had never known before. His heart swelled with the beauty of it, just as it did when he listened to a symphony orchestra playing Mozart, for example, or read a particularly fine piece of poetry. What, after all, could compare with the dizzy blue vault of the sky overhead and the throbbing rhythms of insects as they crawled, hopped, skipped and jumped through the great jungle of grass, weeds and wild flowers? Nothing!

Nothing, that is, except to have all of that *and* someone else your own size with whom to enjoy it. Mo was kind and very loving, but she wasn't a mouse. The glass from which she drank her milk was large enough for Arvee to drown in! Still, he was very grateful for her company. She never allowed anyone else to handle him, for instance, and she was always mindful of his dignity.

Other than Mo, the only living contact he had was with flies, spiders and a few mosquitoes. He had been back to the floor at night a few times, exploring. He told himself that it was part of his thesis on human habitation.

On one of these visits, he met a pair of slow, gentle beetles who seemed to be quite willing to come up and keep him company in his home. They were both shiny black with narrow heads and they were about the same size, relative to Arvee, as a Labrador is to a human. They didn't talk, but when Arvee tickled them just behind their necks they gave out a soft, humming sound, their antennae trembling delicately with pleasure.

Arvee fed them scraps from his table and they quickly grew accustomed to waiting beside him, twiddling their antennae, begging to be fed. He called them Whee and Hum for the slight differences in the tone each produced.

One night, as Arvee was leaving his study to go to bed, Whee suddenly gave the most unexpected chirp. She (or was it he? Arvee couldn't tell) raised herself high on her six spindly legs and her antennae went rigid, pointing in the direction of the front door. 'What is it, Whee?' said Arvee. 'Do you hear something?' Whee chirruped again. Clearly there was nothing to be done but to go and find out.

Both the beetles followed Arvee, their antennae tense, as he went to investigate. And sure enough, even before he reached the door, Arvee could hear a faint scratching.

But when he opened the door and looked outside, there was nothing to see. The familiar tabletop stretched emptily away, the shadows of the plastic trees fell with neat regularity and the benches had the lonely look of a park at closing time. 'Well?' said Arvee to Whee. 'Seems like you were wrong, eh? There's no one here.'

Just as he said this, he saw a slip of something white, a piece of paper that had been folded and pushed under the front doormat. Arvee picked it up. 'B WAY R' it said, twice, in big scrawled letters: 'B WAY R'.

Arvee scratched his head in puzzlement. 'Bee? Way? Ar? What on earth does that mean?'

It took him several seconds to work it out. 'BE-WAY-AR! "Beware" – spelled all wrong. How very odd! Who could possibly want to warn me about something?'

It had to be from someone who was just learning to write, but he didn't know anyone of that description. Which meant it was from someone he hadn't yet met. 'And how did this message get here, anyway? And what must I be wary of?'

There were no replies. From high up on the ceiling, a lizard called, with its guttural 'TCH-TCH-TCH-TCH'. It seemed to be mocking Arvee. 'Look at you,' it seemed to be saying, 'in your fine mansion all alone, with only two beetles for company!'

Just then Arvee heard a creak. He knew that this meant the door to Mo's bedroom was being opened because he recognized the sound. But no one had entered the table-room. No one he could see from his front door, that is.

Moving so that he was hidden by the shadow cast by his house, Arvee edged round the outside wall till he was facing towards Mo's room. If he wanted to see anything on the floor, however, he was going to have to stand up on one of the park benches. He felt glad that he had put the light off in his study. He wouldn't have liked being silhouetted against it now, as he climbed on to the nearest seat.

He peered into the darkness. Sure enough, there beside the bedroom door, on the floor, was a huge, unfamiliar shape.

Alphonso!

It had to be him. Since the time of his first meeting with the Stringers, Arvee had checked with his books. He knew a little more now about the handsome, purring carnivores that humans kept as pets. Mo had apparently shielded Arvee so thoroughly from the cat that he'd not had so much as a whiff of the creature's presence. Until this moment.

Arvee crouched down at once. He realized for the first time how much more practical it was to be brown, like Ellie, Stringer and the rest. He knew that his white fur made him far more visible than any of the others would have been in his position.

Alphonso's large head was raised towards the table.

Arvee could almost feel the cat's eyes raking him. He remained where he was, not daring to move but, surprisingly enough, he didn't feel frightened. Not really. He knew what he was supposed to feel, but his heart was beating quite normally. He was thinking clearly and logically. 'Perhaps,' he told himself, 'if I'd grown up with a fear of cats, I'd be rigid with terror now. But since this is the first time I've seen one, all I feel is curiosity. Even though I know that he . . .'

Alphonso began to move.

He was perfectly silent. He crept forward into the moonlight coming in through the window and Arvee saw at once that he was a beautiful creature – his thick fur was a rich, orange-gold colour, though muted by the cold bluish light. A human would have known his breed to be Persian. To Arvee he seemed more like a moving carpet.

Then Alphonso craned his head to see the table better. During the day his eyes were pale yellow and the pupils were thin slits down the centre. But at night his pupils widened hugely so that the moonlight entering his eyes just then caused them to flash like twin mirrors.

Arvee felt as if two spotlights had been trained on him.

There was no doubt now that the cat had seen him! But Arvee was calm. I'm too far from my front door to run for it, he thought, so my best bet is to stay put.

The cat was crouching, getting ready to launch. Cats see well at night because of a chemical called Visual Purple, thought Arvee, recalling the article he had read a few days ago. Nevertheless their nervous system is triggered by the movement of prey. In clinical trials they have been shown to lose interest in prey that remains still for a long enough time . . . so . . . the best thing for me to do is stay absolutely still! Until the exact moment when he jumps. Because he'll have to take his eyes off me then and . . .

And after that? Do the one thing he won't expect, theorized Arvee. His mind was still perfectly calm. Run in the direction no other mouse would run – towards the cat!

So that's what he'd do.

There's still the question of what to do then, thought Arvee. The choices are to jump off the table or to –

The cat sprang.

9

CAT-ASTROPHE!

Several things happened all at once.

Exactly as Alphonso leaped up to the table, there came from Mo's room a startled gasp. 'Arvee!' she called. 'Arvee is that you? Oh, you *naughty* mouse! Have you escaped?'

Arvee had no time to wonder why she said this. He dashed towards the table's edge just as the cat's great, white underbelly arched over him. He caught a terrifying glimpse of outstretched paws with claws extended like scimitars. Then he reached the table's edge. Alphonso landed with a heavy thump on the table. But, before Arvee could leap down to the floor, he was whacked sideways by some enormous thing. It was Alphonso's huge tail, swishing wildly, as the cat momentarily lost his balance from skidding into the plastic trees.

Arvee was swept right off his feet and landed with great force, *thwack!* against his own front door. His breath was knocked clean out of him. For a few seconds he couldn't move so much as a whisker. The feline will get me now, he thought, in that strange, calm way, right now, right this minute, while I'm too winded to move . . .

But Alphonso too remained frozen where he was, on top of the table, staring at the bedroom door. Mo's voice, calling out so unexpectedly when she should have been sound asleep, had stopped him dead. He willed his little mistress to stay where she was. He absolutely couldn't afford to be discovered at his task – and besides, what had happened to the mouse? It had been right there, just where his forepaws were, but . . . aha! He remembered the impact of his tail on some small thing just at the moment that he reached the table. Quick as thought, Alphonso twisted round, striking with his lethal paws even as he turned.

Too late! The few seconds' delay had been just enough for Arvee to recover. He had crawled quickly in through his front door and bolted it tight behind him.

Whap! Alphonso's paw hit the doormat outside. And *Whap! Whap! Whap!* He battered at the door.

But it was made of good strong teak. It didn't give way. Standing flattened against the wall across from the front door in the small entrance hall, Arvee's heart hammered in his chest. It had been a close call! For how long would the door stand up to the punishment? And if it gave way, could the cat reach into the house with his paw?

Just as these thoughts were going through Arvee's head he heard a shriek from Mo. 'AL-PHON-SOOOOO!' she screamed, from the door of her bedroom. 'ALPHONSO – GET DOWN!' And there came the wonderful sound of Alphonso's claws scraping hurriedly at the edge of the table as he jumped to the floor.

The next couple of hours were rather trying.

All the lights in Paradise Villa were flung on as Mo's parents appeared on the scene, alerted by her cries. The shock of being awakened from her sleep and then of finding her cat attacking Arvee's mansion had been too much for the little girl. She was sobbing hysterically, convinced that Alphonso had swallowed Arvee whole.

Despite his own shattered nerves, Arvee forced himself to come out before Alphonso was made to atone for a crime, which the cat had not, after all, committed. But it took quite a while to attract the attention of the humans. They had decided to concentrate their efforts upon punishing Alphonso, who had squeezed himself under the bookcase, refusing to come out.

Finally Mo's mother caught sight of Arvee, sitting innocently on a park bench, as if surveying the scene without a clue about the part he had played in it. Amidst more tears, of joy this time, Arvee had to submit to being examined for any signs of injury.

The door to the doll's house was also examined as proof that Alphonso had indeed been in the throes of an attack when Mo found him. A broom was produced. Despite terrible spitting and cursing from the frightened cat, he was made to vacate his hiding place. Mo's father, holding him by the scruff of his neck, escorted him from the room.

It was well past midnight before things finally settled down. Mo was given a glass of milk and Arvee made himself look relaxed enough to sit on her shoulder while she gave her mother the highlights of the night's adventure.

'I had a dream, Mama,' she said, 'and in the dream, Arvee was trying to wake me up – but it was such a *real* dream that I *did* actually wake up. And . . . and . . . then I came to see if he was all right and there was Alphonso – oh, Mama! Why did Alphonso do that? He's never killed anything, he doesn't eat meat.' She was still quite tearful. 'He was always such a good cat. Oh why, Mama, why . . .' And her mother tried to explain what she could about cats and the natural habits of predators.

Finally everyone wished everyone else goodnight, plans were made to make the table-room Alphonso-proof and Arvee was able to close his trusty front door for one last time that night.

'What an evening it's been!' he said out loud. Whee and Hum had both come around to meet him, their antennae twittering anxiously. They had scuttled away under the sofa in the drawing room from the time Arvee had found the note under his doormat. He bent to tickle them both in the way they liked. 'Not much use in a crisis, are you?' he said to them ruefully. But he was too fond of them to mind.

He stretched to shake the tiredness out of himself. 'Time to go to sleep!' But Whee and Hum seemed to have different ideas. Instead of letting him go up the stairs and to his bedroom, the pesky beetles kept bumping into him so that he had to stop and say, 'What on earth is the matter with you two?'

Whee chirped and pushed Arvee so hard that he almost fell over. 'Hey, watch out!' said Arvee, starting to get annoyed. But both beetles were pointing with their antennae in the direction of the drawing room. 'D'you mean you want me to go there, then? What funny little creatures you are! Can't you see I want to go up to bed?' But the beetles were absolutely determined to have their way.

'Oh, all right then,' he said in exasperation, with the two beetles crowding him on either side. 'Just to please you.' He moved across the hall and flung open the door.

There was Ellie, curled up on the sofa, fast asleep!

10

NO SLEEP FOR ARVEE

'Ellie!' cried Arvee in astonishment. 'What *are* you doing here?'

Ellie awoke with such a start that she jumped right to her feet. 'Oooh!' she squeaked, in fright.

'Sorry!' said Arvee. '*You* gave *me* such a start that I couldn't help myself!'

'No, no, it's my fault,' said Ellie. 'I'm sorry to sneak into your house like this, without any warning – it's just that I . . . I . . .' Then, to Arvee's utter horror, she sat down on the sofa and started to sob.

'No . . . hey, wait . . . don't. . .' he said. He sat down next to her, with his arm round her shoulders, and patted her paw with his own, till the tears began to subside.

'Ohhh, Arvee,' she said, presently. 'You can't imagine what terrible things have been happening. I've been so afraid and I just couldn't think of anything else to do but . . . but. . . to go and wake the . . . you know . . . your . . . human friend . . .'

'You mean it was *you* who woke her up?'

'I knew about Alphonso. I knew that he was planning to get you tonight and . . . and there wasn't time to warn you or anything. I just had to do something as fast as possible and . . . oh!' She was completely overcome with fatigue and fear.

'There, there,' said Arvee soothingly, patting her heaving shoulder. 'Nothing that a hot cup of chocolate won't solve.'

Ellie jerked her head up. 'No! I haven't explained anything! There's no time to lose! Papa's been taken by the rats, and Toon vanished two days ago, and Moonie's very ill . . . and then I heard this message over the ant network about Alphonso and . . . and . . .'

Arvee, listening to her, realized that things were much more serious than he had thought. 'Don't tell me all at once,' he said. 'You'll only get me confused. First things first: let's get that cup of chocolate. Have you had anything to eat?'

Ten minutes later, Arvee, Ellie and the two beetles were sitting in the friendly little breakfast nook. There was a bit of cream soup left over from dinner and a couple of very tasty baked beans, which Ellie ate wrapped in strips of chapatti. The two beetles were lapping at a bowl of milk and Arvee had his usual mug of chocolate in front of him.

'Now then,' said Arvee, 'start at the beginning and go quite slowly until you reach the end – and please stop apologizing about barging into my home because I'm really happy to see you, even if it *is* the result of a crisis.'

That brought a small smile to Ellie's face. 'It began the day after the last time you came to our house,' she said. 'Toon didn't come home till the next morning.

'Papa was so mad at him! It was awful. Toon said some horrid things, but so did Papa. About what a lazy, reckless, careless mouse Toon is, and how he would be the downfall of all of us, and how he has the wrong sorts of friends, and . . . all of that. It isn't anything new – he's been saying it for a long time.'

'What did Toon say?'

'Oh, he accused Papa of being a stick-in-the-mud. That's when he brought up the subject of you and how we were so lucky to have you as a friend and that if Papa had any brains, he would let you help us. Then Papa found out that Toon had come to see you and that's when he got really wild and boxed Toon on the ears.'

'Oh dear, oh dear!' said Arvee, feeling awful.

'Well . . .' said Ellie, 'Papa's very proud. He doesn't want to feel he needs anybody.'

'What did Toon do?' asked Arvee.

'He vanished. We haven't seen him since then.'

'But where's he gone?'

'To live with his friends, I guess. He's always threatened to do that.'

'Tell me,' said Arvee. 'Where exactly *is* Ratland?'

Ellie smiled wanly. 'On the other side of the house. And underground. This is an old building, so the walls and floors are really thick. Over the years, we mice excavated large apartments all the way inside and under the floors and the walls.'

'Isn't that bad for the building?' Arvee had done a couple of years of engineering, so he understood about these things. 'Doesn't it weaken the structure?'

Ellie frowned a little. 'I don't know . . . we've always just taken the building for granted.'

'Hmmm,' said Arvee, looking thoughtful.

'And then this morning, Papa went out, you know, to look for food. He always goes around three in the morning. But he didn't come back.' Ellie began to look bleak again. 'Mum and I waited and waited and waited. We were both feeling quite hungry and Moonie was crying and Papa still hadn't come back.' She paused to take a breath. 'That's when I decided to listen in on the ant network.'

'How exactly does that operate?'

'Well,' said Ellie, 'all you have to do is stand near the ants, anywhere in the chain, close enough to hear what one ant says to another. Each ant has certain bits of information and as soon as it meets another ant going in the opposite direction, it exchanges its own information for whatever the other ant has.'

'But how do you get to hear something specific?'

'Oh, you can't. You have to listen to all the exchanges. Sooner or later, if there's anything in particular you want to hear – if it's there at all – you'll hear it! Sometimes there are many ants carrying the same message. Then you'll hear it again and again. And in quite a lot of detail, if you listen for long enough.'

'Where and how do the ants *get* the information?' asked Arvee, sitting forward with interest.

'They get the messages from anyone who wants to send them. It's quite simple. You catch one of the ants in the line, feed it a grain of sugar and repeat your message several times – the more times the better. But you have to keep feeding it or else it gets restless and nips at your paws.'

'And how do you know whether it's understood what you've told it?' asked Arvee.

'It doesn't understand a word. It just memorizes the sounds of what you say to it. So you have to be quite careful to say things that won't become jumbled up when they've been repeated by several dozen ants all along the network.'

'My goodness!' said Arvee, enthralled. 'This is really fantastic! A living news network. Does it work well?'

Ellie shrugged, 'It depends. Many of the messages are just silly things fed into the network by the flies and the beetles. Or nonsense sounds that the ants go on repeating long after they've ceased to make any sense to anyone. But it's the only way to communicate across a distance. It's simple and quite cheap – a few grains of sugar. So if you want to hear any gossip, all you have to do is to keep your ear to the network.'

'And that's how you heard about your father?'

'Yes. I stood and listened and within a very short while I began to hear the message.'

'What exactly did it say?'

'Just four words: "Stee-ring-er – held – for – questioning" – that's all. Repeated about once every ten ants, which means that whoever fed in the information must have caught and fed at least twice that number.'

'But who sent the message? The rats?'

'I don't know!'

'And are there any creatures in the house who make it a point to send news messages through the network?'

'If there are, I've never heard of them,' said Ellie. 'On the other hand, I just can't think *who* would have sent the message warning us about Alphonso. Certainly not the rats.'

'What did that message say?' asked Arvee.

'I was listening for more news of Papa when suddenly I heard something which sounded a bit like: "Alf –

Onsoto – Getar – Vitonite". It was so muddled up, I didn't pay attention to it the first time I heard it. But the sounds knocked around and around in my head until suddenly I knew what it meant: "Alphonso – to – get – Arvee – tonight"! And that's how I knew.'

'It could have been a message for Alphonso from the rats.'

'Oh no,' said Ellie. 'Alphonso can't hear the ants. He's too big. No. It had to be someone who knew about the attack and who wanted to warn you.'

Arvee looked thoughtful. 'I had a warning too,' he said. He told her about the 'Beware' message which had been delivered to his doorstep. 'But there's an odd thing. I've not had time to think it through properly until just this minute. The knock on my door was the reason I stepped outside my house and found the bit of paper. At that exact moment, Alphonso came into the table-room . . .'

'But who delivered the message?' wondered Ellie, looking intently at Arvee.

'I worked that out while I was sitting with Mo. It must have been a spider. It could have come down on its silk, tapped at my door and then vanished back up again – I didn't think of looking up at the time.'

There was a silence. It was hard not to feel depressed.

Arvee was the first to snap out of it. 'The thing is, what should we do right away?'

'We have to go home quickly,' said Ellie. 'My mother's trying not to worry, but with Moonie so ill and Gramps to look after . .

'I'll tell you what,' said Arvee. 'Let's pack a basket of food to take to your house, just for the time being. And then we'll shift everyone to *Mercara.*'

'Oh, but . . . it'll be far too much trouble . . .'

'Look,' said Arvee, 'we know now that the rats know about *me*. That means your troubles have become my troubles too.' He didn't tell her that he preferred it that way.

11

FIGHT OR FLIGHT?

In the drain house, only a few of the pistachio-shell lamps were still burning. The small room was dim.

'Is there any way,' said Arvee, looking up at the ant line running along the ceiling's edge, 'of asking the ants for information?'

Ellie was holding Moonie, while Ding sat with Gramps, feeding him from a bowl of mashed baked beans. Ellie said, 'We've never tried to do that.'

'For instance,' said Arvee, trying to answer his own question, 'supposing we fed a question into the network, anyone who knows the answer could send an answer out.'

'Ye-e-s,' said Ellie, uncertainly. 'But everyone who listens to the network would hear the question then . . .'

'. . . including enemies,' said Arvee, 'but we can't help that. On the other hand . . .'

'What do you want to find out?'

'Where your father is being held, for one thing. Oh, and I have another question about the ant line: how can I get the ants to bring the line up to *Mercara*?'

Ellie's ears twitched in embarrassment as she shook her head. 'I don't seem to know *anything*, do I? We've never really asked ourselves such questions . . .'

'Well, never mind, then,' said Arvee. 'I'll tell you what. I'm going to settle down with this packet of sugar I have with me and feed messages into the ant line right now. Let's see what happens!'

It was tedious but simple work. Standing on a stool Arvee would pluck an ant out of the line, hold it gingerly by its delicate waist and quickly stuff a grain of sugar into its clacking jaws while reciting a short message several times. The ant would struggle very slightly – then, after a pause, in a strange metallic voice without any tone or emotion, it would repeat the message.

The sound didn't seem to come from its mouth at all but from its antennae. 'Where – Is – Stringer,' it repeated and, 'Ant – Line – Needed – In – *Mercara*'. Then it would clack its jaws to ask for another grain of sugar. After it had repeated the message correctly at least three times, Arvee would put it back in the line and it would resume its course as if nothing at all had happened.

In this way, Arvee fed two messages into the ant line to at least fifteen ants each, just to be sure of making himself well heard.

'So that's that,' he said, stepping down from the stool. 'I wonder how long it'll be before the message circulates all the way across the line?'

'But we're not going to be here to listen to the line,' said Ellie. 'We're going to be in your house.'

Ding's quiet voice came from the rear of the room. 'I'll stay here with Gramps and listen,' she said. Her voice, despite its softness, was firm. 'I've been thinking. I believe Gramps won't survive the trip to Arvee's house. I can't really take Moonie either, he's too weak. You two go. And I'll stay tuned in to the network.' It was a very painful decision but, whichever way Arvee looked at it, there didn't seem to be any other solution.

'OK,' he sighed. 'You've got a point. For the time being, and only because we can't think of anything better, that's what we'll do.'

Ellie was very quiet as she packed a small kitbag of things to take with them.

Soon it was time to leave. Rather than prolong the unhappy moment, Ellie gave her mother a quick nuzzle, then went over to where Gramps sat and gently wished him goodbye. She patted Moonie briefly between the ears as he lay in his walnut-shell crib. Then she fled down the corridor towards the drain.

Arvee turned to bid Ding goodbye. 'We'll come back every three hours or so from tomorrow morning,' he said, 'to check on the news and to bring food and supplies – one good thing since Alphonso's attack on me has been that he's locked in Mo's parents' room and can't come out on patrol any more!' He was trying to be cheerful.

Ding smiled, 'I can't thank you enough for what you're doing,' she said. 'I feel sure, now that you're with us, things will be better.' And she waved Arvee on his way.

As he turned the corner down the passage he glanced back into the room. He saw Ding wipe her eyes, and then climb on to the stool to start her vigil at the ant line.

All the way back to *Mercara*, Arvee's mind was working furiously. Even though Alphonso was not a threat any longer, it was hard to predict what the rats would do next.

I wonder why they set Alphonso against me, he thought, again and again. It was so strange to think that creatures who were themselves so powerful could feel threatened by one individual animal, and a mouse at that. What makes them think I can harm them?

Arvee showed Ellie to the guest bedroom, downstairs by the study. 'Keep the curtains shut,' he cautioned. He was well aware by now that Mo might not be delighted to see mouse-guests staying in *Mercara*. Humans were certainly unpredictable. The same people who shrieked at the sight of brown mice were willing to hold Arvee in the palms of their hands and exclaim, 'So sweet!'

He went upstairs to bed feeling so tired he barely had the energy to brush his teeth, comb his whiskers and massage his delicate pink tail with moisturizing cream. He tickled Whee and Hum a couple of times before climbing under his sheets and falling sound asleep.

12

ANTASTIC!

Arvee awoke from strange dreams of giant rats, and armies of ants marching along holding flags and banners.

It was five thirty. He could hear Mo moving about in her bedroom, getting ready for school. She usually came to check on him before she left at six. She also used that time to replenish his stores of food. He wondered when she would begin to notice that he was suddenly using up all his supplies. He would have fallen asleep again if he hadn't heard an unfamiliar sound. Very, very soft, like a kind of continuous, tiny pattering.

He sat up quickly. Looking around, he saw that Whee and Hum were also alert, their antennae rigid and their narrow heads lifted up towards the ceiling. Following their gaze, he looked up too and saw – the ant line!

Arvee practically vaulted out of bed. 'The network! It's come here! That means someone *must* be directing the flow of ants!' How else to explain the promptness with which he had been sent a connection? It seemed like a miracle.

He set a chair and a plaited-cane stool against the wall so that he was able to reach up high enough to listen in. At first, just like Ellie had said, there was only a lot of nonsense. 'Eeep – Ouuuut – Eeep – Ouuuut,' said one ant in its mechanical voice and, 'Gookoo – Gookoo – Gookoo – Gookoo!' said another, while a third was full of foraging advice: 'Cake – Crumbs – Tea room – Stop – Dry – Chapatti – Kitchen – Window – Stop,' and several others were full of sounds which were probably from insects: 'Deet – Bleep – Tlikka – Zdwing' or 'Brrgrr – Qughatook – Mrtyuuum – Jtkta – Jtkta – Jtkta.'

The exchanges took place so fast that Arvee hadn't been listening for long before he heard something interesting. 'Arvee,' said the ant in its unreal voice, 'Arvee – Arvee – Arvee.' It seemed to be a message for him! Or was it random noise, like some of the other ones?

How frustrating not to be able to ask questions, thought Arvee to himself. But he realized that, to some extent, his question about the ant line had not only been answered, it had been acted upon. And promptly. So it's just a question of waiting, he thought.

Sure enough, some thirty ants later came the first sign: a scrambled version of his own message. It sounded like: 'Wez – Stee-Ring – Er,' but he recognized it immediately. And what seemed to be the answer, following close behind, was much clearer: 'Coming – home – coming – home.'

The thrill of hearing an answer was so great that Arvee wanted to run right down to Ellie to tell her. But better sense prevailed. He realized that so long as the ants were carrying answers close to the source question in the line, he should stay and listen to whatever else might follow.

Gradually, the full message, three ants deep, came through. When the whole message was strung together it said: 'Stringer is coming home.' 'He is well.' And then, most strangely, 'Exchange for white mouse.'

Arvee listened long enough to satisfy himself that there wasn't anything else. Then he got down from his perch near the ceiling to puzzle it out. Why would the rats demand an exchange of Arvee for Stringer? First they tried to use Alphonso to get rid of him, and now they wanted him alive.

There was only one explanation. The rats wanted to isolate Arvee from the Stringer family. It was a cunning way to destroy the friendship: by creating a conflict of loyalty. If Arvee hesitated to go, it would mean that he cared more for his own safety and comfort than for the whole little family that depended upon Stringer.

Arvee decided that the first move was to go downstairs and make something for Ellie to eat. The second move was to send out his response, as well as another series of questions, on to the ant line. 'I won't tell her about the connection,' he thought. 'I don't want her to feel obligated to me. It's *my* decision to go.'

Ellie seemed a little subdued over breakfast. Arvee gobbled his down and dashed back to his room as soon as he could. He set about putting a message out with furious haste. He had thought of a method of speeding up the process. First, he plucked three ants off the ant line all at once. Using cotton thread, he tied each unwilling insect to the legs of his big brass bed.

Then, while Whee and Hum looked on with interest, he produced three bowls of sugar, one for each ant. He let the creatures gorge to their hearts' content on the sweet grains, then settled down to feed his messages to them.

He had devised three simple ones. The first was, 'White mouse accepts exchange'. The second was, 'Explain Alphonso's attack'. The third was, 'If imprisonment, then for how long?'

Having already eaten their fill of sugar the ants were in a calm and happy mood. Sitting close to them Arvee noticed that they looked a bit dusty, especially compared to the lacquered appearance of his two beetles. To give himself something to do, Arvee got out a tin of black shoe polish and a dust cloth. He began to polish each ant as he read out its message to it.

And what a response he got! Instead of merely parroting the words, the creatures practically sang them out, their antennae waving in tune. And what's more, they each learned all three messages.

By the time Arvee felt they were ready for release into the line, the three ants were gleaming. Within seconds they were absorbed into the line and had vanished from Arvee's room. He had no idea how long he'd have to wait for a response.

Going over to his bedroom window, Arvee looked out over the pleasant vista of the tabletop, the plastic trees and all the rest that was now so familiar. 'What will I do about Mo when I am with the rats?' he wondered. On the heels of this thought was a more melancholy one: that he might not survive to see the Stringer family actually reunited. After all, the rats had set Alphonso on him. There was no reason to assume that he would be safe with them. But at least I'll have done something for the Stringers, thought Arvee, feeling noble.

His years as a scholar, his breeding, his education – all of these had trained him to be philosophical about life and death. He had enjoyed his life in the Laboratory. His day's routine had been regular and filled with activity. If someone had asked him then if he were happy to be alive, he would have answered unhesitatingly, 'Yes!'

But here . . . it was different.

At his window, his paws neatly folded behind his back, he couldn't help but feel that life alone in *Mercara* wasn't really worth a beetle's hum. It was comfortable, of course, and interesting and adventurous. But . . . lonely. In the end, the loneliness made everything else seem unimportant. Maybe that was why it was easy to agree to be exchanged for Stringer.

A sudden, furious knocking at his door broke into the stream of his thoughts. Not waiting for a response, Ellie burst in.

'Arvee!' she cried. 'Arvee – I just heard your message on the ant line.'

'Which . . . what . . . ?' said Arvee, momentarily confused.

'The ant line – don't you see, it runs all over the house,' she said, looking up to check where it ran through his room. 'I saw it in my room first thing this morning and I listened to it. When I heard about . . . about . . . the *exchange* I prayed that you'd not noticed the connection! That's why I didn't say anything to you when I saw you at breakfast. I didn't want you to go.'

Arvee smoothed his whiskers back. 'Let's think this through carefully.'

'No! I have it all worked out! I could go in your place, you see –'

'No, you can't! You're not white.'

'The rats have never seen you up close, so all they know is that your fur is white. If we cut my hair, and change the colour of my fur . . .'

'And how would we do that?' asked Arvee, smiling at the thought. 'Surely it can't be as easy as you make it sound?'

But it was Ellie's turn to smile. 'At last! Something I know which *you* don't!' She told him that in the mirror cabinet in Mo's bathroom, there was a big bottle of laundry bleach. 'You see, my great-aunt – the one who was so simple-minded – once fell into a cup of bleach. It turned her fur completely white for almost two months!'

Arvee looked alarmed. '*Bleach?* That's hydrogen peroxide! I'm sure it can't be good for your skin. It'll burn – might even cause blisters . . .'

'Oh, Arvee!' exclaimed Ellie. 'They've got my *father*! A little discomfort is nothing compared to that – I mean, I know that my great-aunt was OK except for the shock and the looking . . .' She was going to say 'bizarre' but stopped herself in time. She didn't want to hurt Arvee's feelings. 'Different.'

'But – but . . .' Arvee spluttered. 'You don't imagine for one instant that I would let you go in my place?'

'Why ever not?' said Ellie. 'I may as well tell you, I've already tried your clothes on. I got a few out from your laundry bag and they fit perfectly. As for cutting my hair, that's easy too.'

Arvee looked at her, speechless. Here he was, getting ready to be the great hero, and meanwhile Ellie had worked everything out for herself! 'Um . . . let's think slowly and methodically . . .'

'No, no, there isn't time. It's the only way! If you go, your little human will miss you.'

Thinking very quickly, Arvee said, 'Yes, that's right, but supposing we combine both the plans? You change the colour of your fur and stay in *Mercara*. Meanwhile, I'll go to the rats. If they get suspicious about a second white mouse in *Mercara*, I'll explain that I *had* to leave a decoy in my place or else the humans would turn the house inside out, searching for me.'

'How's that any better than my going?' asked Ellie.

'Well, look: for your father, it'd be terrible to return from Ratland only to find that *you've* gone instead – don't you see? It'd seem too high a price.'

Ellie tried to protest. 'But you – '

'No,' said Arvee. 'I think this is better than anything else we can think of.'

'What about the colour of your eyes, then? My eyes are black. Surely your little girl will notice that?'

'I have sunglasses,' said Arvee. He fished them out at once from his dressing table and handed them to her. 'I always wear them when we're sitting out in the garden because the sunlight's too strong for my eyes. It's only during the day that she'd notice the colour of your eyes, if at all. Here, try these on.'

Ellie put the sunglasses on her nose, turned to the mirror and started to laugh. 'Oh, how *funny* I look!'

Arvee smiled. 'It's so nice to hear you laughing for a change.'

13

BATTLE PLANS

So it was agreed that Ellie would take Arvee's place while he went to the rats. The morning passed in delivering supplies to Ding and discussing the plans.

When they were back in *Mercara,* Arvee had a little time to show Ellie around. As they entered Arvee's study, she gasped. 'Oo! So many *books*! Have you read them all?'

Arvee tried to be modest. 'Well, not *all* . . .'

Ellie was silent. She picked up a couple and leafed through the pages, put them down, looked at some more. She seemed to be thinking of something. Abruptly she turned to Arvee and said, 'Is it . . . *difficult* to learn to read?'

'Oh no – it's the easiest thing.'

Ellie looked away.

'You can learn on your own, actually,' said Arvee. 'I could just start you off and I'm sure you'd pick it up in no time.'

'Oh – could you? Would you?' cried Ellie, so enthusiastically that Arvee had to smile.

'Your father wouldn't like it, you know,' he said.

'My father will have to get used to some changes,' said Ellie, her ears twitching back in that determined way she had. 'He needs to see that learning new things isn't entirely wrong.'

'But why does he think that at all?'

'Because of the other mice, the ones in Ratland. The ones who work for the rats.'

'Have you ever met them?' Arvee wondered what she would think about Toon's news of revolt.

'No.' Ellie was silent a moment. Then she looked at him, a serious expression on her face. '*You* will, though, in just a short while – which reminds me: we should be listening to the ant line. Maybe there's a message about you.'

There was. It came later in the day, five ants deep. 'Stringer to return tonight.' 'Dr Arvee to await instructions.'

'Ah, it's "Dr Arvee" now!' said Arvee.

'Cat attack a mistake.' 'Not imprisonment.' 'Length of stay optional.'

'Optional?' said Arvee to Ellie. 'How can they say that?'

Her ears twitched. 'Typical of the rats! They use words in the exact opposite way to what they mean.'

'Why d'you suppose they want to meet me?' asked Arvee.

'No idea, except it can't be anything good.'

As soon as it was dark, Ellie and Arvee ran down the table's column and wriggled into Mo's bathroom. 'We have to get up *there*,' said Ellie, pointing to the mirror cabinet up above the basin.

Both mice were fully prepared for the occasion. Ellie had cut her hair and was dressed in Arvee's clothes. She had four thumbtacks tied to her belt, in pairs, with their points tucked under opposite caps. She also had a towel and a large sponge tied to her back. Arvee looked like a cross between a mountaineer and an archer, with two long plastic straws and one short one held across his back by a length of bicycle-valve tubing. A long coil of embroidery-thread rope was tucked into his belt.

A friendly spider took the rope up to the basin, looped it round one of the taps and came back down again. 'You go first,' said Arvee to Ellie. 'I'll hold both ends down here, firm. Once you've tied a knot up there, I can join you.'

Soon both mice were on the rim of the glistening white basin. 'The bottle's in the cabinet behind the mirror,' said Ellie, looking up. 'Thank goodness no one bothers to shut it. Look! Can you see that brown glass bottle? At the front of the lower shelf? That's the one.'

Once more the spider went ahead of them and looped the rope round the top of the bottle. Ellie clambered up.

Behind the bottle was a box of detergent. Standing on its firm, flat surface, she pushed her tacks into the side of the shelf. When she had anchored the rope to the tacks, she called down to Arvee, 'Ready!'

He climbed up the rope. 'Now,' she said, when he was standing beside her on the detergent box, 'this is the hard part: unscrewing the bottle cap.' Arvee and Ellie gripped opposite sides of the plastic bottle cap and pushed with all their might.

It had no effect at all.

'Oh no,' said Ellie. 'It's shut tight!'

'Think slowly and methodically,' said Arvee. 'Don't panic or lose hope. Perhaps if we sit on this detergent box and push with our feet? Come on! Let's hold on to the rope, wedge our heels into the grooves on the bottle cap and push together . . . one, two, three . . .' Almost immediately they felt the cap move.

Two more turns and it was loose. Arvee took it off and set it down on the detergent box. There was a stopper in the mouth of the bottle. Arvee levered it off and immediately the powerful smell of bleach filled the air.

'Are you sure that's all you'll need?' said Ellie anxiously.

'That' was the device Arvee was wearing strapped to his back. 'We'll just have to see,' he said. He took the two long straws off his back and gave them to Ellie to hold, while he tucked the short one into his belt. He untied the rubber valve-tubing and fitted it on to the long straws so that they were now connected to one another. Then he got one straw into the bottle, while the other one dangled down the side of the bottle and out of the cabinet.

'You better get the soap-dish cover in place,' said Arvee. 'I'll be ready very soon!'

Ellie climbed down the rope to the edge of the basin once more. The plastic cover of a soap dish was close by. She turned it up so that it formed a shallow basin and pulled it over to where the end of the second of the two long straws dangled. 'Ready!' she called up, as she caught the end of the straw and held it over the soap-dish cover.

Now Arvee took the short straw out of his belt. It had a pointed tip and was about two centimetres long. 'I'm going to pierce the rubber valve-tubing with this short straw. Then I'm going to suck up the bleaching liquid.'

'But how will it get down into the hanging straw?' asked Ellie.

'I don't have time to explain in detail, but it's a simple siphon. Once the liquid comes up as high as the top of the bottle, it'll automatically flow down into the lower straw and into the soap-dish cover. And it'll *keep* flowing down till I break the connection between the straws.'

So saying, Arvee carefully inserted the pointed tip of the short straw into the valve-tubing. He put his mouth to the blunt end of the straw and started to suck upwards on it.

It took a few tries to get right. He sucked the bleach up inside the first long straw, then into the valve-tubing and then, with just a bit of jiggling, he got the liquid to flow down into the second long straw. In the next instant, bleach began to pour from the bottle and into the soap-dish cover.

'It's flowing, it's flowing!' cried Ellie excitedly. 'Just like you said – it's like . . . magic!'

Arvee sat back, feeling pleased. 'Elementary physics, actually,' he said, wanting to give her a properly scientific explanation for why the bleach rose in one pipe and flowed down into the other.

'Oh, never mind the physics just now!' said Ellie. 'To me it looks like pure magic.' She waited till the dish cover was almost full, then called up, 'Enough, I think.'

Arvee pinched the rubber tube shut, breaking the connection between the two long straws. The flow of bleach stopped.

'OK!' called Ellie. 'I'm going to get in.' So saying, she stripped off her T-shirt and jeans and climbed into the soap-dish cover. 'It does sting a little,' she called up to Arvee, a few moments later. 'But not painfully. The smell's much worse!'

'Is there enough bleach?'

'I think so. When I lie down full length, I'm completely covered. How long d'you think it should take?'

'I'm timing you,' said Arvee. 'According to the instructions on this bottle, not more than ten minutes. But be careful! Don't get it in your eyes.' He wished he hadn't agreed to this wild and far-fetched scheme! He also hoped, for Ellie's sake, that she was doing a thorough job. 'Is the sponge working?' he called.

'Well, I'm fixing my whiskers now.' Her voice faltered. 'And . . . yes. They're . . . they're coming out *white*. Oh, Arvee! I'm sorry – I don't mean to sound rude, but it *does* feel weird to have white whiskers . . .' Arvee felt a twinge of pain inside. So even Ellie thinks I look strange, he thought, sadly.

When the ten minutes were up he called down to Ellie to tell her so. 'I'm ready,' said Ellie. 'Every part of me that I can see looks white!'

Arvee heard her step out of the soap-dish cover and towel herself dry. Presently she called up, 'I'm dressed!'

Arvee looked down and saw – a white mouse. 'My goodness,' he gasped, 'it really works. You're absolutely white!'

14

JOURNEY TO THE UNKNOWN

The two mice left the bathroom as they had come. Back in *Mercara*, there was a painful moment when Ellie stood in front of the mirror in Arvee's room and saw her complete self for the first time.

Her whiskers trembled. She touched her ears and the sides of her nose as if she just couldn't get used to the idea that the reflection in the mirror was really hers. Her eyes, huge and dark against the whiteness of her fur, glistened, though she didn't cry. She turned to Arvee and said, 'You know . . .' Then she stopped, as if searching for words.

Arvee's feelings were in turmoil. To him, she looked perfectly normal. It was a peculiar relief, in fact, to see another mouse who resembled him. But to her, obviously, it was a terrible disfigurement. Like losing her tail or an ear.

'You know,' she began again, 'I had no idea it could make such a difference to my appearance.'

'Well, with luck, it won't be for too long,' said Arvee. He couldn't help it if he sounded rather stiff. The hurt he felt was similar to the time when Stringer had told him that they could no longer meet. But worse. Because this time it was Ellie.

Ellie heard the stiffness in his voice. She thought it was because he was regretting having got mixed up with her family and their endless problems. Like her father, she was proud. She didn't know how to deal with the overwhelming sense of guilt that Arvee's generosity had left her with. Rather than discuss her feelings with him, she asked, 'Do you think your little human will recognize that I'm not you?'

Arvee shrugged and said, 'She'll think you're me because you're a white mouse and because you're in my house. Humans can't tell the difference between mice until they've got to know us very well.'

Ellie put on Arvee's spare sneakers, tucked a couple of pens into the pocket of her T-shirt and smoothed back her hair the way Arvee did. Now she looked exactly like him! Despite the sadness they had both been feeling inside, looking in the mirror they were soon giggling. But it was getting late. 'It's time for me to go now,' said Arvee.

'Don't forget to feed Whee and Hum, and don't shrink away when Mo holds her hand out to you – remember, she's used to me being very friendly with her.'

'I'll try my best, Arvee,' said Ellie. 'I guess it was a good thing that I was the one who woke her up when Alphonso attacked you, because at least I have *some* experience, now, of being close to a human.'

'I don't know how you had the nerve to do that,' said Arvee. In all the excitement since then, he had forgotten the enormity of her courage. She'd never been in contact with a human before, yet she'd gone all alone to wake Mo up.

'It was *very* difficult, but I knew nothing else would stop Alphonso. So I made myself do it.'

Arvee felt a sudden lump forming in his throat. The moment of departure was at paw now. Whatever else was true, he was going to miss Ellie. 'Well, erm, I'd best be off,' he said. They were standing by the escape-hatch in the drawing-room floor. 'Remember to keep this properly closed at night and don't open the front door to anyone.' He prised up the bottle cap and got ready to go down. 'Goodbye – and take care of yourself.'

'Bye-bye, Arvee – take care, you too – and listen in to the ant line whenever you can. And . . . and . . .' Kneeling down impulsively, she very lightly and quickly touched her nose to Arvee's. 'Come back soon.'

When Arvee reached Ellie's house, he found that Stringer had already returned. He was looking thin and tired, but very, very happy to be back. He seemed quite speechless with all the news that Ding had given him. He had no words left with which to thank Arvee. He knew that Ellie would be waiting to meet him, looking very different, in *Mercara*. 'I don't know what to say,' he said to Arvee. 'How can we ever repay you?'

'There'll be time for all that later, Stringer. What I need to know right away is this: where do I go to meet the rats?'

A shadow crossed Stringer's face at the mention of the rats. His whiskers drooped as he said, 'Arvee . . . I can't let you do this for me – don't go! We'll leave Paradise Villa, we Stringers, we'll go far away . . .'

Arvee was shocked at the suggestion. 'No! There's no going back on my word. Tell me what I should do.' He tried to make it sound as if he felt easy and confident.

It was a simple arrangement. There was a cricket sitting on the inside of the drain, awaiting his command. As soon as he told the cricket he was ready, it would leap away to alert its masters, the rats. Arvee was supposed to station himself on the far side of the bathroom, by the door to Mo's bedroom, and wait.

'I think I may as well go at once,' said Arvee.

Stringer was looking haunted. 'You don't know what they're like! They'll twist your mind, they'll destroy you from the inside . . .'

But Arvee only said, jauntily, 'Don't tell me! It's only because I *don't* know what lies ahead that I can bear to go.' He bade Ding farewell. Stringer walked with him down the narrow passage towards the drain.

They reached the end of the passage. They shook hands, then threw formality to the winds and embraced one another. 'Take care,' said Stringer. 'Take care, my friend . . .'

After contacting the cricket, Arvee waited by the bathroom door. His mind was blank. He didn't know what to expect. He heard a faint rustling behind him. Then: the smell of another animal!

A voice, low and husky, addressed him. 'Dr Arvee, I presume?' followed by, 'Don't turn round! I'm going to blindfold you, if you don't mind.'

Arvee didn't resist. A soft cloth was slipped over his eyes, then tied behind his ears. 'Allow me to introduce myself,' said the voice. 'I'm Odd-Tail.' Arvee felt his paw being shaken courteously, held by one that was similar to his but much bigger. Almost twice the size. From the slight heat that all warm-blooded creatures give off, Arvee could sense the height of the animal in front of him, taller than him, and more bulky. A rat.

'It's quite a distance,' the rat was saying, as they started to move. Arvee was guided with a paw on his shoulder. Their route took such twists and turns that even Arvee, with his experience of mazes, was confused. They were inside the walls of the house. Then the path turned downward. Suddenly, the surface underpaw changed sharply, becoming soft and springy. The air changed too, becoming more dense. An artificial, flowery scent lay like a blanket over the normal animal smells.

Arvee felt dreadfully uneasy. He kept himself calm by concentrating on his breathing, as if he were doing a yoga exercise. Whatever lay ahead, he told himself, he must remain cool-headed and rational.

At long last they stopped. Odd-Tail was asking someone if he and Arvee had permission to enter somewhere. Permission was granted.

There was a click, like a door being opened. A whoosh of air greeted them as they entered a large space, followed by a burst of sound: music, conversation and the clink of crockery. The room was absolutely full of other creatures, Arvee realized, all taller than himself, all rats.

Then he heard excited whispers calling for silence. The conversation in the room ground to a halt. The music stopped on a strangled chord. Arvee sensed scores of curious eyes and ears turned in his direction, while he stood blindfolded and helpless.

'All right, Dr Arvee,' said Odd-Tail, his voice suddenly loud in the silence. 'I'm going to take your blindfold off.'

He did so.

Arvee gasped.

15

RELIEF — AND HORROR

The room they had entered was huge and lavish. Every surface was covered in rich silks and brocades. Brass urns had ornamental mushrooms growing out of them. There were statues of rats mounted on pedestals. Hanging from the ceiling were wire cages inside which brightly coloured beetles buzzed and clicked.

A fountain played in the middle of the room and the small pool in which the fountain stood had tadpoles in it, swimming lazily about.

The rats!

There must have been about seventy of them in the room. Like the Stringers, they were dark-furred, but the resemblance ended there. Jewels glinted from the ears and paws of all the females, who were swaddled in silk and chiffon. The males wore fancy turbans and sashes, loose-flowing pantaloons and strings of polished sand grains.

All the males were hefty and well fed. Some carried weapons tucked into their waistbands. Everyone was drinking and a few, Arvee noticed, seemed also to be trailing wisps of smoke in the way that humans did when they used cigarettes.

There were mice too in the room. They were all wearing uniforms, with caps between their ears and gloves on their paws. But, strangely enough, they didn't look at Arvee at all. Some were standing against the wall, observing the scene impassively. Others were clearing away small dishes of snacks or bringing in new ones, while yet others carried trays of drinks.

Right in the centre of the room, lying on a sofa covered with brocade cushions, was the Rat Lord.

He was a giant of a creature, larger than all the other rats present. He was dressed in a fine silk kaftan. His black fur was thick and glossy. He had a vast belly that filled out the contours of his loose-flowing robe. His whiskers had been treated with some shiny stuff, so that they glittered. Pearly beads hung from his neck and turban.

Two little girl mice, rather scantily clad, were waving butterfly-wing fans over him. Another two were massaging his legs and tail. One sat near him, holding his drinking cup and another, next to her, held the nozzle of his hookah.

The Rat Lord was looking at Arvee with the same unabashed openness as all the other rats. Unlike them, however, he didn't seem in the least surprised. He was smiling broadly. His large, black eyes, moist and kohl-lined, seemed to be smiling too.

'Good . . . evening,' said the Rat Lord. What a voice he had! Smooth as treacle, deep and hypnotic. It was the kind of voice which, once heard, wasn't forgotten in a hurry. 'How very delightful to meet you, Dr Arvee. What a rare privilege it is to have a world-famous celebrity in our rough midst!'

Tweaking the ear of the nearest girl mouse, he said, 'Refreshments for our honoured guest!' The mouse scampered off. 'You must be tired after your long journey but, before you retire to your suite, I wonder if you could spare a few minutes to chat with us?'

Arvee stammered, 'Why . . . er . . . yes, of course.' He was dazed. He'd expected to find the rats brutish and uncouth. But, instead, they were the height of sophistication. Was this the Rat Lord who had stormed Paradise Villa and sent Alphonso on a murderous mission? Impossible to believe! The darkness and despair of the past few days were beginning to seem like a distant nightmare, unreal and unimportant.

The Rat Lord entertained Arvee as if he were a visiting foreign prince.

'Call me Pasha,' he said grandly. 'For years, our little community has needed a scholar such as yourself. It was so kind of you to come.'

'But . . . I'm sorry, uh . . .' said Arvee.

'Pasha,' prompted the Rat Lord.

'I don't quite see what use I can be to you,' finished Arvee, wishing he didn't sound so lame.

'Why!' said Pasha, looking astonished. 'So much! My dear Doctor, you have no idea how long I have waited to meet someone as learned as yourself.' He seemed so earnest. 'We rats have known for some time that there are others like ourselves, in the scientific community. But alas, we and they . . . there's no connection. You scholars live in another world. A wonderful world, let me hasten to add. A brilliant, thrilling world. What I would do to be able to claim even a tenth of your knowledge!' He sighed, shaking his huge head from side to side.

'So when I heard about you, I was electrified – yes, that's the word. I thought to myself, now *there's* an animal who can be of outstanding service to us. Don't you see? We need basic skills here, in our little community. Reading, writing and arithmetic, and at all the advanced levels too. If you were willing, I could let you start an educational foundation! I'd give you all the funds you need, all my resources would be at your disposal!'

Arvee was feeling dizzy with food and drink and relief. He wondered if anyone present knew how to make a good hot cup of drinking chocolate. 'I – I'm not the right mouse for your purpose,' he said, humbly. 'You see, my training was a little too specialized . . .'

'Oh, come on, Doc,' said Pasha. 'Don't be so formal! Just teach my people what you know, and we'll gradually find other scholars and thinkers to come and lecture . . .'

To be sure, it was a tempting proposal. To be actually in charge of an education policy for the rats! He could introduce them to all kinds of ideas. Ideas that might change their entire way of life. Classical literature, poetry and art, history and biology, physics and chemistry . . . He felt so sure that if only animals had access to higher education, they would automatically learn to behave decently towards one another . . .

'Well, uh, well,' he said, smoothing back his whiskers, 'it's all so sudden, you see . . .'

'Good heavens! What a boor I've been, such a graceless, thoughtless vulgarian!' exclaimed Pasha, sitting up so suddenly that the girl mouse at his tail was thrown off balance. 'I've kept you here, discussing these trifling matters without the *least* thought for your comfort! A change of clothes, a shower and a nap – my dear sir, how can I begin to apologize?' Before Arvee could say or do anything else, he found himself being escorted out of the audience hall by a girl mouse who had been assigned to him. 'Show him to his suite!' Pasha said to her. 'Show him all the comforts!'

With that, the audience was over.

Arvee and the girl mouse walked a long distance through velvet-lined corridors before arriving at an ornately carved door. All along the way, the girl mouse had walked on ahead without looking back and without saying a word. Now she unlocked the door and held it open, her head bent down.

It was a generously proportioned room, even by rat standards. On one side was a large desk and a bookshelf full of encyclopedias. On the other side there was a magnificent bed with lace curtains round it. In the bathroom was a grand bathtub made from a human-sized porcelain sauce boat. And in the wardrobe were clothes for every occasion. Arvee saw that they had been made to fit him.

The girl mouse had gone into the bathroom ahead of him and turned on the hot water to fill the tub. Standing at the door to the room, Arvee looked in at the inviting sight of the rising steam. He said to the girl mouse, 'Thank you, Miss, I'll do that myself.'

She looked up at him and stepped away from the tub, but didn't leave the room. Instead, she stood with her head meekly bowed, as if awaiting orders. A little put out, Arvee said, 'Uh, excuse me, Miss, but what I meant was, you may go.'

She stood there, shaking her head. Thinking that this was very odd behaviour, Arvee said, 'Didn't you hear me? I said you may go.'

She shrank back a bit, but didn't leave.

Arvee couldn't understand this at all.

'What's the problem, Miss?' he said, genuinely concerned. He moved towards her, but she squeaked and stepped back, as if in terror.

He stopped. He held his paw out to her. 'Look,' he said. 'Don't be frightened. Just tell me what the matter is.'

The mouse stepped backwards again. Water had started to spill from the tub and she slipped, falling with a cry. It was a strange, twisted sound.

Arvee came forward quickly to help her up and caught her wrist. At this, she started to turn and pull away, gasping in what seemed uncontrollable fear. That was when Arvee realized why she wouldn't answer him. She didn't have a tongue!

Arvee was able to calm the mouse down finally. But he was deeply disturbed by her condition. It was clearly something done deliberately, perhaps as a punishment. If so, it was an extremely cruel one. Unable to talk, unable to read or write, the little attendant was incapable of communication. She couldn't tell him, for instance, about the plight of the other mice in Ratland. Nor would she be able to carry messages from him to anyone else. He had no way of knowing whether she was an exception or whether all mouse attendants were similarly mutilated. He didn't dare speculate upon the fate awaiting Toon and his rebel friends if they were caught by the rats.

Arvee persuaded the young mouse that she was to lie down and sleep if she wanted to, on the divan at the far end of the room. She wasn't deaf, and understood his speech, once she got over being afraid of him.

When he had bathed and dressed for the night, in pyjamas that fit him perfectly, Arvee put out the lights. He drew back the curtains round his bed and slipped in between the silk sheets. Despite all the luxury, however, he knew he wouldn't sleep a wink. 'What does Pasha *really* want from me?' he wondered silently to himself. 'And what will he do when he finds out that I'm not willing to work for someone who cuts out the tongues of poor little mice?'

There was no one to answer his question.

16

PASHA'S PEOPLE

The next morning, Arvee was taken on a tour of Pasha's domain.

First there was Pasha's own residence with its endless rooms, its swimming pool, its ladies' quarters and its nursery: Pasha had more children than he knew how to count. Later, they visited the homes of some of the prosperous rats in the neighbourhood, walking along well lit passages lined with cement and chips of tile.

'You have electricity,' observed Arvee, 'and running water.'

'We have a very good connection with the power and water lines of Paradise Villa,' said Pasha.

Just then, they came to a row of thick iron bars which were set into one of the outer walls of Paradise Villa. Pasha paused to show off the view this gave him of the human courtyard beyond the grille.

Suddenly . . .

KER-RACKATTA-TACKATTA-ACKATTA-ACKATTA-ACKATTA-ACKATTA-BOOM!!!

Pasha and Arvee were tossed against the wall by an explosion just beyond the bars!

KERR-ACKATTA-ACKATTA-ACKATTA-ACKETY-ACK-ACK-ACK!

Acrid smoke filled the narrow passage. Arvee's delicate nose ached from breathing it in. Dizzy with the noise and the shock, he just lay where he was, wondering whether he was about to die. Then he saw that Pasha, though thrown off his feet, had crawled away from the bars. He gestured to Arvee to follow him. Somehow, they both managed to reach the end of the passage and practically fell down a steep incline.

'Cracker season!' gasped Pasha, when he got his breath back. They were both sprawled on the floor. It was the first time that Arvee had seen the rat looking less than dignified. His chest was heaving and his huge whiskers vibrated wildly. 'Dratted fireworks! How I hate them!' He bared his great, yellow fangs in anger against the humans under whose house he lived. 'Humans never seem to understand the effect those horrible things have on us animals!'

'But . . . why do they do it?' asked Arvee, when he could manage a breath or two. 'Is it a war? Are they attacking one another?'

'Nahh,' said Pasha with a contemptuous wave of his paw. 'It's something to do with the cold season coming on, and the shorter days. Humans go a little insane.' He got to his feet. 'It's a weird phenomenon and it happens every year. The name they have for it is "Diwali". You might want to make a study of it some time.'

Soon they were on their way again. But the crackers had forced them off the course they had been on. Arvee was surprised to notice they were in a more seedy part of Ratland. Some passages were unlit, the dwellings were crowded close together, there was a smell of rotting garbage. As they passed the entrance to one of these passages, Arvee could hear drums and mouse voices singing. He asked, 'Who lives in this area?'

'Nobody,' said Pasha, dismissively. 'Servants, peons, laundry workers . . .'

'Oh,' said Arvee. 'Aren't we going to visit them?'

Pasha looked at him, amazed. 'Visit the mice? Whatever for, my dear fellow?'

Arvee smoothed back his whiskers. Pasha didn't think of Arvee as a mouse at all, it seemed! 'I . . . uhh . . .

had the idea that you were planning to train some of the mice as well and I thought it would be instructive to visit their homes.'

Pasha's ears twitched back. 'Hmph! Well! I'll have to see about arranging that some other time.' But from the way he said it, it didn't sound likely that 'some other time' would ever come.

Three days later, Arvee had just come back from yet another lunch party in his honour and was sitting unhappily at his desk. I'm losing my grip on reality! he thought. Everywhere he went, he was fed rich food, entertained with games and admired for his knowledge.

He knew he could not trust the rats or Pasha.

And yet, and yet . . . They were so extravagantly friendly! They took such an interest in his learning! Could these be the same animals that Stringer had warned him about?

It was only when he asked about his mute mouse attendants that he caught a glimpse of Ratland's dark side. There were two of them who took turns serving him and they were the only mice he was permitted to be alone with. He had asked Pasha about these two unfortunates, but initially his question was ignored. Finally, this morning, Pasha said to him, 'They were born that way, my dear fellow. They're perfectly happy, really, but they can't tell you that, can they?' He laughed. 'Don't waste another minute of your valuable time thinking about the poor wretches – here, have another pastry.'

Sitting at his desk, thinking back over this conversation, Arvee felt the difficulty of his situation like a heavy weight across his shoulders.

'But what *can* I do?' he asked himself. 'I don't even have an ant line running through my room! I have no way of communicating with the outside world. It's like a cage made of gold,' he sighed. 'If I'm not careful, I'll get so used to it, I won't be *able* to leave.'

Later the same afternoon, Arvee had been invited to address a gathering of lady rats at their monthly club. The audience hall was packed. Arvee ascended the small platform that had been erected for him. His appearance was greeted with a pandemonium of shrieks, squeaks and applause. Arvee didn't even need to prepare a speech. The audience had endless questions to ask about his family life, the social atmosphere in the Laboratory and whether there was any chance for their children to find good jobs in such a place.

By the time tea and snacks were served, Arvee was quite exhausted. But there was a variety programme. He was given a seat in the front row. On the platform an earnest girl rat was coaxing mournful sounds out of a violin. Arvee's attention began to wander.

There were, as usual, many mice in the room, as attendants. None of them looked directly at Arvee. He gazed at them nevertheless, wishing there was some way he could cross the divide that separated them. He was just thinking this thought for the nth time, when he realized suddenly that one of the mouse attendants was looking straight at him.

Not merely looking, but staring.

This unnerved Arvee. He smoothed back his whiskers. To his surprise, the other mouse imitated the gesture. Arvee scratched his chin in consternation – and so did the other mouse! Arvee decided he was probably imagining things and looked away, with his arms tightly folded. But from the corner of his eye, he noticed that the other mouse was also standing with his arms folded!

For the next few minutes, Arvee experimented with small, fidgety gestures, to confirm that the attendant mouse was mirroring his moves. Then, abruptly, the attendant did something different. He held up a paw as if to say 'Enough!' Reaching into the front of his uniform jacket, he brought out something small and white, a piece of paper. The mouse held the paper for an instant, before returning it to his jacket-front. Nobody else noticed the movement. They were all watching the stage. Then the mouse relapsed into the same state of indifference that all the other mice affected.

Whatever could it mean? Arvee was so fascinated that he almost forgot to clap when the young rat's violin recital was over. At last the meeting ended. Arvee was escorted out by countless lady rats who came up to be introduced, to comment on the elegance of his white fur and to hope that he would come to their homes for dinner.

As he and a small knot of ladies were moving out, Arvee noticed the oddly behaved mouse again, standing near the door. His ears were tense. Nearing him, Arvee saw that the attendant was holding the piece of paper in his paw. *It must be a note!* guessed Arvee. And it looked as if he was expected to pick it up. As he passed the mouse, he took the paper and popped it into his pocket, all in one smooth motion. It happened so quickly, with Arvee talking brightly all the while, that no one noticed a thing.

Back in his room Arvee was desperate to read the note. The mute boy mouse was in the room, however. Conscious that the attendant could be a spy for Pasha, Arvee sat down at his desk and drew up his stack of notebooks, as if settling down to some work. Secretly, he pulled the note from his pocket and smoothed it out in front of him.

There was a drawing of a clock with the hour hand at seven. In large, block letters were two words: 'OUTSIDE ROOM'. The handwriting was block-like and clumsy, in the style of someone just learning to write. A memory tickled Arvee's consciousness, but he didn't have time to examine it.

It was five o'clock. 'So I have two hours to decide whether this message is genuine or . . . not,' Arvee told himself. The best he could hope for was that Toon had discovered a way to be in touch with him and had sent this message through his friends. If not, it meant that it was a trap set by Pasha, to see just how submissive his white-furred prisoner really was. What should Arvee do?

The boy mouse was sitting perfectly still, looking down at his paws. This was how he sat unless Arvee wanted something. What will he do, wondered Arvee, if I go to the door and open it? Would he ring a bell? Run to fetch others? And what would happen if he succeeded in raising an alarm before I got away? What would Pasha say or do to me?

However, there was no point in worrying. Arvee had a leisurely bath and a nap. At ten minutes to seven he changed into the clothes he had worn when he arrived in Ratland. He looked around at his suite. All the softness, all the comfort. Unlimited food. The promise of heading the education project of his dreams. Then he looked back at the sad, mute mouse and his stomach turned. Nothing is worth such a price, he thought. I must go!

He collected the few things he'd brought with him: his torch, a couple of pens and some paper. His watch showed a few seconds to seven. Here goes nothing, he thought, as he strode purposefully towards the door. Opening it quickly, before the boy mouse could intervene, he stepped outside.

17

ESCAPE!

Moving slowly down the corridor was a mouse wearing the white uniform of the sanitation staff. He was pushing a large laundry basket on a cart.

Arvee, standing at the open door, could see from the corner of his eye the boy mouse watching him anxiously. Will he try to stop me? he wondered. Just then he noticed that the key to the room was in its lock. Quick as thought, he grabbed the key, closed the door and locked it from the outside.

The moment he did this, the white-clad mouse leaped forward to hold the laundry basket open. 'Arvee – quick! Get in! It's me, Toon – there's no time to lose!' Still clutching the key to his room, Arvee hopped neatly into the basket, landing on top of a pile of bed sheets and table linen. The lid of the basket was shut tight over him. 'Hide under the sheets,' said Toon.

Phew! thought Arvee. *Now* what?

For a long time, there was nothing for Arvee to do but stay very still, covered in dirty laundry. Toon moved as fast as he could. Finally they came to a halt. Arvee felt the basket being lifted off the cart and dragged a short distance. Toon lifted off the lid. 'Are you all right?' he asked. 'Come on, it's safe.'

Pushing aside the bed sheets and pillowcases, Arvee vaulted quickly out. 'Toon! I can't tell you how glad I am – '

'Shhh! Not so loud, please,' said Toon. He was a changed mouse since Arvee had last seen him. His hair and whiskers had been shaved. The white sanitation uniform hung loosely on him, as if he had lost weight. But there was no time for greetings. 'Here – before we go anywhere, smear this hair dye on your fur and put on this uniform – quick! The alarm will be raised at any moment!' He handed Arvee a bottle of brown hair dye and a sanitation uniform.

They were in the place where all the rats' laundry was collected before and after being washed. Ten or twelve baskets of the kind Arvee had recently travelled in were standing on neatly marked squares on the floor, numbered for the houses from which they had come. In minutes, Arvee's fur was coffee brown. Looking at his transformed arms reminded him of Ellie. It's not a bad feeling to look different, he thought to himself, but it's certainly a strange one! It's exactly as if I had stepped into someone else's skin. If this was how she'd felt being bleached, perhaps he needn't feel so unhappy about her reaction.

'Your whiskers, Arvee,' said Toon, critically. Then he stepped back, a faint smile on his face. 'Sorry, I can't help smiling – you look so much like one of us now!' Then he frowned again. 'Oooops! I almost forgot the contact lenses.'

'The . . .?'

'Contact lenses – to cover your eyes. Here, put them on – no, wait, I'll have to do that for you.' He brought out a container that had two compartments. In each there was a floppy sort of thing, a bit like a small cap, dark brown in colour, floating in a liquid. Holding Arvee's head gently but firmly, and telling Arvee not to blink, Toon neatly transferred each lens to the surface of Arvee's eyes.

'There – do they hurt in any way? Can you blink?' asked Toon.

'Hmmm – no, they don't hurt at all,' said Arvee, looking up and down and all around him. The whole world had turned a nice shade of brown. 'What an extraordinary invention. Are there so many mice who need to change the colour of their eyes?'

'Mice can't afford them,' said Toon. 'They're used by fashion-conscious rats, to turn their eyes blue and green and multicoloured. We managed to get our paws on a pair and dipped them in a strong tea solution to dye them this colour. But, if you'll pardon the informality, let's get a move on!' So saying, he bundled Arvee's old clothes into a shoulder bag. Then both mice hurried out of the room.

Because of Arvee's altered appearance, no one stopped them or asked any questions. Along the way they were joined by two more mice in sanitation uniforms, introduced as Feather and Happy. All four moved along, eyes downcast, as if busy with their work.

Soon they were in a part of Ratland that had been excavated from the bricks of Paradise Villa's outer walls. It was so narrow that the mice could only squeeze through in single file. The rats could not have followed them even if they had wanted to.

They came to a section of rusted pipe. Toon held up a piece of rough sacking that covered the entrance and all four mice ran into the pipe. Arvee could see a light up ahead and then they entered a small room, formed out of a T-junction in the old pipe. At least twelve other mice were already present. There was a pause before Arvee was recognized and then a muted cheer went up. The famous captive was free!

One by one the mice introduced themselves. 'Call me Zero, sir,' said the one who seemed to be the informal leader of the little group. 'We're very honoured to have you amongst us.' Then she looked at Toon. 'But how are things outside? Are we safe?' Toon drew in a long breath. 'We don't have much time . . . they'll be looking for a white mouse, and they'll surely send the Squad after us. I'd give us half an hour. If we're lucky.'

Arvee blinked. 'The "Squad"?'

'The Roach Squad,' answered Zero. 'Trained cockroaches who can track down an animal with nothing more than an eyelash for a scent. They're ruthless . . .'

'They'll take a while to track him,' said Happy, one of the two mice who had been along with Toon. 'The laundry basket would have covered his scent well enough.'

'Still, Toon's right. We have at most half an hour,' said Zero.

'It's too early to take him back via the water pipes,' said a mouse called Lucky. 'It's only eight o'clock, you know. The pipes between here and the table-room will all still be full of water till the humans go to sleep.'

'Just a minute,' said Arvee. 'Did you say "table-room"? Does that mean you're planning to take me back to *Mercara*?'

Zero was young, tough looking and plainly dressed, in grey overalls and sneakers. Using her most businesslike tone, she said, 'Well, yes, sir, if that's all right with you.'

'No – it's not!' cried Arvee, his whiskers bristling. 'Now that I'm here, I can't just leave! What about the resistance movement? What about overthrowing the rats? I thought that was what this was all about!'

Toon looked at Zero. She was shaking her head. 'Sir,' she said, 'Toon told us that you were sympathetic to our cause – but . . .' she looked around at the small group, 'frankly, I don't think there are enough of us to start a revolution yet.'

'Not a revolution, maybe,' said Arvee. 'But . . .'

Zero was shaking her head again. 'Sir, we know you mean well and yet – look what happened when we tried to send you a warning. We wanted to tell you about Alphonso, but the rats intercepted the note, delayed its delivery and almost got you killed.'

'Ah!' said Arvee, 'The Midnight Message.'

Lucky said, 'We can't afford mistakes of that kind.'

Toon said, 'My first attempt at writing . . .' He grinned. 'My second was the note you got today.'

Arvee said, 'So *that's* what I recognized this afternoon – your writing! Bravo! I'm proud of you.' He looked around at all the young faces. How early in their lives they'd had to make adult choices! 'My friends, if not that night, then some other night the rats would have sent the cat. Your message got me wondering about who had really sent it – and why – and how. So it was tremendously useful and it's brought us all together too, don't you see? As for returning me to my house – there's no point. Pasha, the Rat Lord, can always arrange to have me captured again.'

'Then what do you suggest for your own safety, Arvee?' asked Toon. 'You can't stay in Ratland once the

Squad are on to you! We can change your appearance but not your smell.'

'I can't stay anywhere, is the point,' said Arvee, as he smoothed back his whiskers. 'If they can get me here, they can get me there too. So that leaves only one option . . .'

Just then there was a faint crackling sound from a section of the pipe beyond the junction. Two mice, Sparx and Crax, had been sitting apart all that time, listening in on a radio set. It was a larger version of the gadget Toon had had with him the time he visited Arvee. Sparx called out, 'Transmission coming through!'

All the mice crowded around the radio. Buzzes, chirps, clicks. 'I had it just now,' said Sparx, twiddling knobs expertly. 'Ah – here we are . . .'

A rich, unmistakable voice filled the little room. It was Pasha. Arvee felt a shiver run up his tail. There was something about that voice which, even over the radio, cast a spell of trust and confidence – even now, when it was distorted with rage. 'I want him found!'

Pasha was thundering to someone. 'Within the hour! We can't afford to lose that mouse!'

'It's about you,' murmured Sparx to Arvee.

One of the other rats was speaking. 'Sire,' he said, 'we're doing our best . . .'

'Fool!' screamed Pasha. 'Your "best" wasn't good enough to keep that animal safely in his room! He's in the hands of the rebels, I tell you! They don't deserve him! He's different! He's special . . . and I want him for myself!'

Arvee felt his hair stand on end. All the while he'd been in Ratland, the one thing he hadn't understood was Pasha's interest in him. Now, finally, he was going to find out.

Pasha's voice softened. 'When that dimwit Alphonso first talked about the creature, it sounded as if he might be a nuisance. Befriending the Stringers indeed.

'But when the feline idiot bungled his attack and the humans themselves came to the rescue of the tiresome little freak – ah, *that's* when I understood his worth. What power! What glory! A mouse who commanded the protection of humans!' Here he cackled at the thought. 'With a mouse like that working for *us*, who knows what heights we could reach?'

Then his tone hardened again. 'But instead – you fools – he was stolen away! Snatched! *My* special mouse, *kidnapped*!' His voice had become a ghastly shriek, 'I'll teach you to be slipshod! To be careless . . .'

Into the little room entered the most horrible sounds, of gnashing and thrashing, of squeaks and pitiful moans, as Pasha vented his fury on some unfortunate rat.

Sparx turned the volume down. 'We won't hear much more for some time now,' he observed. 'In this mood the Rat Lord can't say many actual words.'

Arvee was numb with horror. He had known the power of Pasha's dangerous charm. It sickened him to think how close he had come to surrendering to it.

18

A THRILLING RIDE

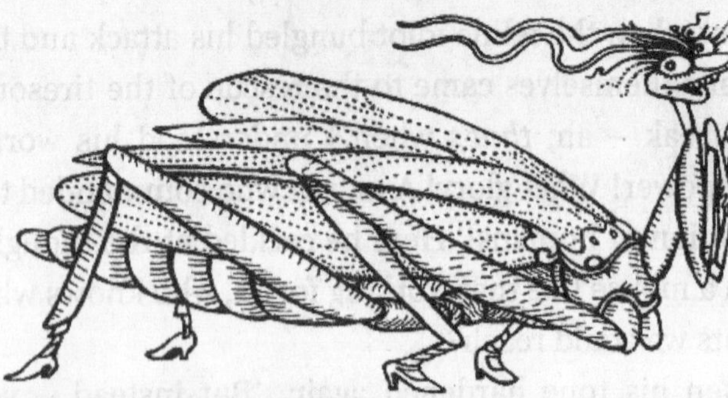

I think,' said Arvee, when the echoes of that awful scene in Pasha's audience chamber had died away, 'this makes it clear. Whatever hesitation I had before this moment, now there's none whatsoever.'

He looked around at the others. 'My fellow mice, we have no choice. We must get rid of the rats . . . altogether.' Toon looked at the floor. Zero was silent.

Arvee smiled. 'You think I'm talking through my whiskers, don't you?' he said. 'But I have a plan that I think *will* work.'

Zero said, 'Sir, you've seen how they punish mice.' She made a slicing motion with her paw, across her tongue. 'Those two in your room were young trainees in our group. When they were caught, they had two choices: get their tongues cut out or . . .' She shrugged, rather than complete her sentence.

Arvee nodded. 'I understand. So, quick! Let me tell you my plan. If you think it'll work, we'll go ahead. If not – I'll make my own way back to the table-room. I don't want any of you risking your lives for me. Agreed?'

Zero started to say, 'Agreed, but – '

Just then Arvee jumped. 'Ooh! What was that? There's something on my leg!' The other mice leaped to their paws. 'It's here,' said Arvee, bending and twisting comically. For a moment it looked like he had gone a little mad. 'No, here now. Here – oooh! It tickles.' Then, all of a sudden, they saw what it was: an ant!

'Good . . . gracious,' said Arvee, holding it up by its slender waist so that he could look at it properly. 'What are *you* doing here, little one?'

Zero said, astonished, 'That's incredible! An ant? All on its own, not connected to the ant line? I've *never* seen that happen!'

Arvee said, looking at it closely, 'You know, I do believe this is one of the ants I polished. See? It's still quite shiny.' In a few words he retold the story of how he'd sent his message back to the rats.

'Still, that doesn't explain what it's doing here now,' said a mouse called Heavy. He jumped. 'Oops! Here comes another one!' And then one more. The three that Arvee had fed and pampered in his house were soon gathered together on the small table around which the mice were standing.

Once assembled, the group of special ants twiddled their antennae and recited their message in unison: 'Use – Us – For – Private – Messages!' they said in their unnatural voices. 'Message – Delivered – To – Animal – Of – Choice!' and, 'Reply – Guaranteed – In – One – Hour!'

And having said that much, they repeated themselves till Arvee petted and stroked them. Upon which they sat on his shoulders, twittering softly.

The other mice were so astounded by this performance that they could only stand and gape.

'Oooh! Don't tickle!' said Arvee as one of the ants twiddled its antennae curiously inside his ears. 'This is wonderful. It's *exactly* what we need to help our plan along! Where was I? Ah yes, but there's one thing I need to know, before I start . .

The rest of the mice were looking at him expectantly. One or two had uncertain expressions on their faces and he couldn't tell precisely what they were thinking. He knew that it was by no means certain they would go along with his plan. Nevertheless, he had to try.

Smoothing back his whiskers, he asked, 'My question is, what do you know about . . . firecrackers?'

Two hours later, Arvee and Heavy were standing on a step leading from the kitchen to the back garden of Paradise Villa.

It was a new experience for Arvee. I've never been out at night, he realized. He had seen the stars and the night sky from the Laboratory of course, but here, out in the open, it was very different.

Human noises had died down, but the night was alive with the sounds of insects. In the grass and in the air, like a swirling carnival of movement, six-legged creatures were everywhere, dipping, swaying, buzzing along, flittering and crawling, or just moving slowly and moodily through the grass. Over and around them were the swiftly darting forms of bats as they swooped around catching their breakfasts – because of course, for them, the night was when they woke up. Above the bats, occasionally, and moving more slowly than all the other creatures in view, there might be the silent form of an owl looking for someone tasty to catch.

Heavy, however, had no time for any of the sights and sounds on display. He was turning his head this way and that, looking for something specific. He took out the little torch Arvee had given him and started to flash it. 'She usually takes a little while,' he said to Arvee, 'but let's hope she's in a good mood tonight.'

'Why do you flash the light?' asked Arvee. 'Wouldn't whoever it is come quicker if you kept the light steady?'

'It's Madonna's code,' said Heavy but, before he had a chance to explain himself, there was a turbulence in the air. A gigantic shape loomed above them in the darkness and a great whirring of wings stirred up a storm of dust.

Heavy wasn't afraid. 'Here she comes!'

In the light of his torch, Arvee looked up and almost fainted with fright. An enormous praying mantis was poised in the air, her glittering eyes staring down at Heavy and him.

The gale from her wings reminded him of the table fans humans used in the summer. Instead of the whirring of machinery, there was the crackling rattle of insect wings. A moment later, she had thumped down on the step, in front of the mice. Her throaty, clickety-clack voice boomed down to them. 'Well, hellooooo, boys! What can Madonna Mantis do for you tonight?' Then she tossed her triangular head in the air and said, 'SSSSSssss – chk-chk-chk-a-chk-chk-chk!' all the while flapping her long, spiked and dangerous-looking forearms in front of her. She was almost fifteen centimetres long. 'Put your hands together, boys, and pray along with the Mantis!' she cried, with a wild, mad laugh.

'You're going to send me off on a – a – *praying mantis*?' asked Arvee, shouting to make himself heard above the din of the thing's wings as they thrummed the air. 'I'll never make it – I'll fall off – I've never flown before in my life.'

'Come on, come on, boys!' she called down, sending the upper part of her body rearing up. 'Madonna's feeling hungry for fun tonight! She wants to get her snack and do some fancy flying!'

Heavy said, 'Relax, Arvee – it looks worse than it is, trust me.'

And the odd thing was, he was right.

A few moments later, Arvee was sitting astride the broad abdomen of the insect, with two loops of rubber band strapped around Madonna's giant back legs, for him to cling on to. 'Just hold tight to the straps,' said Heavy, 'and you won't fall off. I'll follow you just as soon as I can catch another mantis . . .' He had already fed Madonna the first part of her fee, which was a strip of old ham the rebels kept just for occasions such as this one. He gave another strip of ham to Arvee. 'She knows the way, but you must be sure *not* to pay her before you get there, whatever she says. Or else . . . you never know! She can be a bit, well . . .'

'Mercenary,' she cackled, in her loud voice. 'I'm just a material girl, after all! Gotta work for my living. All riiiiiiight! Are we all strapped in back there? Good! Now where'dja say you wanted to go? Clear around to the other side of the house, huh?'

She gave a bounce and then – up! She was airborne. Arvee almost fell off right away, with the jerk. 'It's a long flight, Mister Mouse – I just can't be sure I'll make it without that second payment along the way!'

'This – is – crazeeeeeeeeee!' squeaked Arvee, pulling on the rubber bands for dear life.

But the night sky spun above him, the air whirled and thundered around his ears. There was no one to answer him. The mantis's head was quite some distance away, since she was a long-bodied insect. Inflight conversation wasn't very likely. Beneath him Arvee could feel Madonna's abdomen, firm and springy, the texture of strong, thick stalk. The fat cylindrical body expanded and contracted rhythmically with the creature's breathing.

Arvee had heard about people being airsick and he wondered if he would be. They were going so fast and the earth seemed far below. What an unbelievable adventure this was turning out to be! When he thought back now to his life in the Lab, it seemed to him that the difference between then and *now* was the same as the difference between standing still and running as hard and as fast as he could, but there was still so much dangerous work ahead.

'How're we doing back there?' boomed the voice of the praying mantis. 'Wanna pay me a little something for my trouble right now? Wanna get off and take a pit stop? Wanna see the sights? Just say the word . . .'

'I'm fine,' shouted Arvee. 'Just get me there safely!' Hanging back on to his straps, he shut his eyes and thought – So long as I don't think about what I'm doing, I can almost believe it's fun!

19

THE CRACKER CAPER

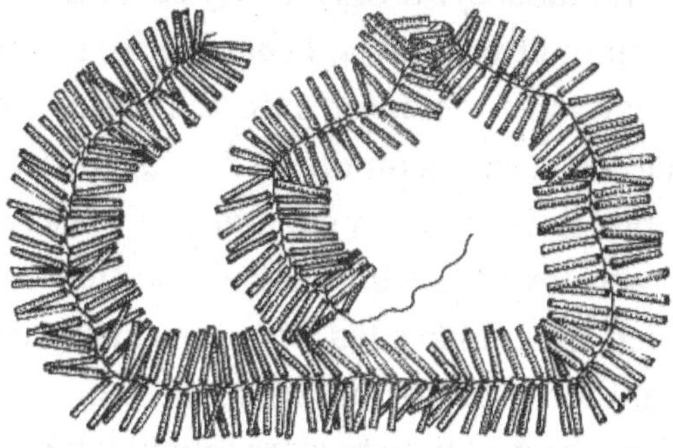

They arrived with a bump that shook Arvee almost off his seat – and woke him up. He'd fallen asleep mid-flight!

'Come on, come on!' called the booming voice of the mantis from high overhead. It took Arvee a couple of seconds to be properly awake. 'Can't wait all night! Us working girls gotta keep flying or else . . .' She trailed off while making a dangerous-looking cycling motion with her fearsome forearms. Arvee didn't want to imagine what exactly she meant by it.

'Sorry!' said Arvee, scrambling off quickly. He managed to glance at his watch – it looked like they hadn't taken so long after all, maybe twenty minutes at the most. He hoped Heavy had managed to find himself a mount too.

'Here you are, Ma'am,' he said politely, holding up the strip of ham to the huge creature towering over him.

Madonna stooped swiftly, grabbed the ham from Arvee's paws and sprang up in the air. 'Hooooo-eeeeeeee! Thanks, little mousey! If only all my customers were so prompt with their payments, I could retire in comfort!'

With that she zoomed off into the night. Arvee felt as if he had been riding on the back of a whirlwind. The night seemed quiet, now, by comparison. He saw that he had been set down on what looked like the top step of three, which should have led from the garden to a door, except that there was no door he could see.

But before he had time to worry about what he would do if Heavy didn't arrive, he heard a sound that he had now learned to recognize: a Mantis Airline flight about to land. He scrambled out of its way just in time, as another giant insect crash-landed on the step.

'That's the last time I carry you, buster!' shrieked this new mantis, whose name was Daisy. Her forearms were sawing the air in an alarming way. Apparently she was talking to Heavy because, a moment later, Arvee saw his friend picking himself up from where he had fallen off his perch. 'Never heard of weight restrictions? I could'a arrived way ahead of that old bag, Madonna, except for Mighty Mouse here, weighing me down . . .'

Heavy just shrugged good-naturedly and unwrapped a long roll of chapatti that he had tied round his waist. 'Here!' he said, 'It's more than you deserve – I was sick all the way.' The mantis snatched her fee and rose straight up in the air. A moment later she was gone.

'Phew!' said Arvee. 'This is a dramatic way to travel!'

'But fast,' said Heavy. 'And it keeps you, sir, off the ground and out of the way of the Roach Squad for just a little longer. Now then! Let's find that door . . .' He darted across to the right side of the step. By sniffing and tapping, he soon found what he was looking for. 'Here! There was once a door in this place, but the humans have boarded it up. There's supposed to be a crack in the plaster for us to find . . .'

Sure enough, screened by tall weeds was a crack in the plaster that widened into a hole. It led from the garden, in through the wooden frame of the blocked door and to the table-room.

'I hope our ant delivered its message to Ellie,' said Arvee.

Toon had said that the Stringers kept this hole blocked from the inside for security purposes. So a message had been sent to Ellie via the personalized ant service, describing how to unplug the hole. I hope she's there! thought Arvee to himself. After all, there had been no news from the Stringers since the time he had left *Mercara*. Suppose . . . ? He didn't want to think of the unpleasant possibilities.

Both mice were at the entrance of the hole now. Heavy hesitated, before turning to Arvee.

'Uhhh . . . Arvee, sir, would you mind going in ahead of me? I've never met Ellie before, you see. I don't want to startle her by appearing before you.'

'Good thinking,' said Arvee and crept into the little hole.

It was overgrown with moss inside. According to Toon, it was a simple straight hole and . . . was that a light he could see at the other end? It was! Calling to Heavy to follow him, he went quickly ahead and, in just another moment or two, he heard Ellie's voice say, 'Arvee? Is that you?' It was all he could do to stop himself rolling over and kicking his paws in the air! It was so nice to hear her voice again.

'Yes, it's me, Ellie,' he called and then he suddenly remembered that she might not know about his changed appearance. What would she say now?

In the next moment, his whiskers poked out of the hole.

'Arvee!' cried Ellie. 'What – ' and then as the rest of him appeared from the hole, 'Arvee . . . is it really you?'

Then, to his great relief, she began to laugh, standing there, wearing his clothes, the perfect replica of his former self. 'What a strange and funny time we've had ever since you came to Paradise Villa, Arvee,' she gasped, when she found her breath. 'Brown mice become white, and white ones become brown and everything . . . upside down!' Then she laughed again. 'See? I'm even speaking in rhyme!'

In a very short while, all three mice were in *Mercara*, drinking hot chocolate. Heavy and Ellie had been introduced, and Arvee would have loved to have gone straight up to his room and a hot bath, but there was too much to do.

'Uhh . . . excuse me, ma'am? Were you able to confirm that the crackers are really in this room?' Heavy asked Ellie. Arvee was surprised to notice that Heavy seemed slightly formal with Ellie. It was the result of her artificially white fur, he realized.

'Yes,' Ellie was saying. 'They came three days ago, in that big carton in the corner there.'

Heavy looked impressed and said to Arvee, 'How *did* you guess they'd be here, sir?'

'When Pasha told me that these things are used mostly by human children, I *knew* that Mo, the young human I'm friendly with, would keep them in this room. This is where she stores things that aren't used every day.' He put down his mug. 'I think we'd better get to that box right away, hadn't we?' He glanced at his watch. 'In another half hour, Toon will be ready for us.'

As all three mice moved towards the carton, Arvee explained the plan to Ellie. 'First I've got to find the right kind of cracker, the kind I saw that day from the iron grille.' They had reached the carton. 'Then we deliver them to Toon, who *should* be waiting for us with your mother and father, just where the back passage from your home opens out to the garden.'

The carton was high, but its outer layer of thick cardboard had worn away in some places, revealing the corrugations inside. For the mice to climb up was as easy as using a staircase. Soon all the three were inside and standing atop a mountain of crackers.

'Now let me see,' said Arvee, surveying the scene. 'The kind I'm looking for weren't in a box . . . and they weren't long straight sticks . . . and they weren't in a pot . . . and they weren't – ah! There they are! That's them.'

He scrambled down to where he saw the beginning of a string of small, red, pipe-like objects just like the ones he had seen that day with Pasha, before they had exploded with that awful racket.

'Thank goodness there are so many of them,' he said. He found the end of the string and passed that up to Ellie, who was standing a little above him, on the edge of a box of sparklers. 'Start pulling, but please be careful. These things are quite dangerous. Heavy and I will get the rest out from under here.'

In a little while, the three mice were standing once more at the top of the carton, with a seemingly endless stream of red crackers piled all around them like the coils of an immense serpent. 'This should be fine,' said Heavy, 'don't you think?'

'Well, I hope so,' said Arvee, 'because it's the best we can do.'

He picked up one end of the cracker line and let it down over the side of the carton. When he had pushed enough over the edge, the weight of those that were already down began to pull the rest of the crackers behind them. In a short while the whole string had slithered down to the floor. The three mice leaped lightly off the top of the carton, landing on the pile of crackers.

'Oh, Arvee,' said Ellie suddenly. 'What's Mo going to do when she finds her noisy toys have gone?'

Arvee smoothed his whiskers back. 'I hadn't forgotten about her,' he said, 'and I don't like to steal; but I'll tell you how I've rationalized it. If she could understand what we're doing, I'm sure she'd be on our side. But we can't explain. We have to take the crackers without asking her permission. Fortunately, there's almost double this quantity still inside the box, so we're not depriving her of them altogether.'

Working methodically, all three mice began to move the string of crackers across the room and out through the hole that led to the garden.

It wasn't easy. The crackers did not move smoothly through the hole and there was always the chance that someone would notice the strange activity taking place on the unprotected, open step beside the boarded-up door. 'Be careful,' called Arvee to the others. 'There's gunpowder inside each one of these. If we're not very careful, there's a chance it will explode. If even one of them goes off now, we'll be badly burned.'

The worst was soon over and the crackers were out, off the step and on the ground.

'You know what?' said Heavy, looking over the untidy heap of little fireworks that now lay in the shadow where the wall of the house met the ground. 'I bet, when we straighten out this string, we'll almost be at the place where Toon said to meet him.'

He was right. In another short while, the whole long string of crackers lay stretched out and, just ahead, they could see the place where the back passage from the Stringer family home came out. It had once been the mouth of an old pipe, now covered and plastered over. But there was a large crack in the plaster. Even from where they stood, they could see a faint light winking within it.

It was Toon, with a torch.

He rappelled down on a length of twine dangling from the mouth of the old pipe before Arvee, Ellie and Heavy reached him. 'Right!' he said, 'I'll take it from here. Uncle and Auntie are both up inside the back passage. The rest of the team are on the roof.'

To Arvee he said, 'No time for details, Arvee, but in brief – the rats are convinced that you're still in Ratland. No one has reported seeing a white mouse anywhere and the Roach Squad continues to be thoroughly confused, following our trail of red herrings.'

Arvee explained to Ellie, 'The others have spread bits and pieces of my clothing all over Ratland, to confuse the Squad.'

Toon handed Arvee a packet that he was holding, 'Here's your wetsuit.'

Heavy joined them but only to say, 'Time's ticking along – we'd better get on with delivering the crackers to the roof.'

Toon said, 'Arvee, if it's all right with you, why don't you and Ellie go on ahead of us?'

'Maybe he needs a rest!' said Ellie. 'Arvee? You've been going all day long – don't tire yourself too much.'

'I slept on the flight, so I'm fine,' he told her. 'I'd rather not stop now – we've got a good lead, particularly if the rats don't realize that I'm no longer in Ratland. I'll tell you more about the plan when we've got to the roof, OK?'

Ellie nodded. They scampered towards the guttering that led to the roof of Paradise Villa. It was easy enough for two young mice to find footholds between the plaster of the wall and the shallow channel of the guttering, which also offered them good shelter from any hungry owls.

Even before they had reached all the way up, Toon had started to follow behind them. Tied to his waist was a sturdy rope, long enough to reach all the way to the roof from the ground. Attached to the other end of the rope was the line of crackers.

20

AN EXPLOSIVE IDEA

The roof! Ellie had never been up there before, not even once. It took her breath away now, the vastness of it, the open expanses of sheer, uncovered whiteness, the great looming shapes of the water tanks and the pipes and . . . and . . . 'Ooh!' she exclaimed, sounding a little breathless, 'It *is* . . . big!'

Some distance away, she could see the small group of Toon's friends standing under cover of the nearest water tank, waving towards her and Arvee. She turned to him now and said, 'You know – there's no time for anything, but I just *have* to say, before we meet the others here, that I'm . . .' she stopped and blinked a couple of times, completing her sentence in a hurry, '. . . well . . . I'm *very* glad to see you're all right!'

Arvee felt himself smiling all over as he replied, 'Oh, Ellie, I'm glad too! And let's hope we'll *all* have reason to be even more glad very soon.'

They joined the others and there was a hasty round of greetings and introductions as Happy, Feather and another mouse, Horse, welcomed Ellie to their midst.

Happy said, 'Everything's set up for you, Arvee – the plastic nose gear, the paper clips, the nylon string and the pulleys so that you can climb up the pipe.' It all sounded mystifying to Ellie, but it was obvious that this was part of a well-laid plan. 'Sparx and Willing also managed to send a message through the ant line, to say that they're expecting to be in place fifteen minutes from now.'

'OK, everyone,' said Arvee, 'that means I have no time to dawdle! Toon will be here soon – and meanwhile I've got to get my balloon in place. Good luck – good luck, everyone, and remember: be methodical, work slowly, don't make mistakes.'

The other mice sped away to await Toon's arrival. Arvee turned to Ellie. 'If you can help me get into this balloon-suit, I can finally tell you about the plot as we go along.'

Inside the package that Toon had handed Arvee were a couple of rubber balloons and also sections of other balloons that had been cut up. 'Now, let's see,' said Arvee, 'these two long bits must be for my legs and . . .' He removed his sneakers and stripped down to his undies. Ellie helped pull the stretchy portions of the balloon carefully on to Arvee's legs and arms. Soon he was covered completely in a suit made of white-spotted blue rubber. The vest portion had been cut in such a way that the mouth of the balloon looked a bit like the polo neck on a sweater.

Ellie gaped at him, trying not to smile. He *did* look funny!

'These rubber bands,' said Arvee, pulling them out of the packet, 'are to ensure that the different sections of the balloon are quite tight and waterproof. Right up to my neck.' He even had four small rubber pouches for his paws so that they were protected too. 'And now, if you were able to find my jar of moisturizing cream –'

'Yes,' said Ellie. 'I have it right here.' She patted her pocket.

'Wonderful,' said Arvee. 'I don't need it just yet – we'd better get to the ventilation pipe first.' He looked around the roof and quickly located what he was looking for. 'See that there? The long thin pipe, sticking up from the edge of the roof?'

They began trotting briskly towards it, taking the precaution of staying within the shadow of the parapet wall. Arvee described the course of action that lay ahead. 'That pipe connects to the main supply of water, which connects to that great big tank there.'

He stopped long enough to scratch a quick diagram in the white plaster of the parapet wall. The water tank was a huge rectangle, with a pipe leading away from it. 'That's the main water pipe. It takes water to the whole house. Toon and his friends, who have a map of the entire plumbing system, say that the first connection off that pipe is to the master bathroom. That's right beside Mo's parents' bedroom.'

Then he drew the ventilation pipe, showing how it connected at right angles to the main water pipe. 'Sometimes a bubble of air gets trapped in the pipe and blocks the supply of water from the tank. The purpose of this ventilation pipe – the V-pipe for short – is to prevent those blockages from happening. If any air gets trapped, it's released when it reaches the V-pipe. But tonight I'm going down the V-pipe in order to create an *artificial* blockage.

They began to sprint forward once more. 'I'll go down the V-pipe suspended from a nylon rope, taking a balloon with me. At the end of the V-pipe there'll be water,' he said, 'which is why I'm wearing this wetsuit. The moisturizing cream is to help me slip down inside the pipe or else I might get stuck. I'll also have the plastic bottle cap that Happy mentioned, to place over my nose in case I fall in the water.'

'Oh! That would be *awful*!' cried Ellie.

'Don't worry,' said Arvee. 'The bottle cap will give me a bubble of air to breathe for just a few moments.'

'But – why are you doing all this?' asked Ellie.

'In a minute – you'll see: when I reach the water at the end of the V-pipe, I'll position my balloon in such a way that, when I blow it up, it'll block the main pipe.'

'But . . .' said Ellie uncertainly, 'what if someone turns on a tap in the bathroom? Won't the water start to flow – and pull you away with it?' It all seemed very risky to her.

'It's night-time now,' said Arvee, 'and the humans usually sleep all through the night. Otherwise, yes, you're right, it *would* be dangerous. Speaking of which, we'd better hurry! Sparx and Willing must certainly be inside the master bathroom by now.'

He ran forward faster than ever, with Ellie trailing behind.

'And – and what are *they* doing there?'

'You see,' replied Arvee, over his shoulder, 'once I've blocked the main pipe with my balloon, they'll open the tap in the bathroom – and that'll make all the water that's *in* the pipe flow out.'

'I – I don't understand.'

They had reached the ventilation shaft. Both mice were panting with the effort of running and talking at the same time. 'The crackers!' gasped Arvee. 'Don't you see?'

'No! It's not making *any* sense to me!'

Arvee caught sight of the plastic bottle cap Happy had mentioned, lying at the foot of the V-pipe. 'Here's my face mask,' he said. A simple pulley system had been set up, made from a pair of empty cotton reels, with the nylon string looped round it. 'And here's our rope. Come on! Once we're up, I'll need your help to get down inside the pipe.'

With the face mask hanging down his back from a loop of rubber band, Arvee began to climb, holding on to the nylon string. Ellie followed him. They got to the top easily and were soon perched on the rim of the V-pipe. It had a thickened lip at the top, exactly as if the engineers who designed it had known that two little mice might need a place to sit while catching their breath in the midst of a daring adventure.

Happy and her team had used this thickened lip to secure another long piece of nylon string and another pair of reels as pulleys. Arvee tied one end of this string round his waist and Ellie was able, with the help of the pulleys, to control his slide into the pipe. Each had a paper clip clapper they could use to clang on the side of the pipe to relay simple messages. Three taps meant, 'Let me down', two meant, 'Bring me up' and four meant, 'I'm untying the string – don't worry'.

'I'll use the moisturizer now,' said Arvee, taking his rubber mitts off. 'You mustn't touch it, or your paws will get greasy and you won't be able to hold the rope.' Ellie watched as he smeared the cream on to his face and whiskers and ears and all over the outside of his suit. Then he put his mitts back on. 'OK, Ellie, time for me to go.'

'But you've not told me what's supposed to happen next, Arvee,' said Ellie, worried. She knew he was in a hurry, but how could she be effective if she didn't have a picture of the whole plan in her head?

'You're right to ask,' said Arvee, 'but I've only got a moment: by draining the water out of the pipes between here and the master bathroom we'll be able to go all the way to Ratland – from *inside* the water pipes! Remember – the rats get their water from a leak in these pipes. That means there's a weakness in the plumbing close to the heart of Ratland – maybe the pipe's cracked a bit, or one of the joints is loose. Whatever it is, once we get down into the pipes, we'll take a parcel of crackers right up to where that weak spot is. And if we can take crackers there, we can light them. And if we can light them – BOOOOM!' He grinned wide. 'Pipe bursts, we unblock the pipe up here and – all the water from that great, big tank will thunder down through the pipes and straight into Ratland!'

'Oh!' Ellie cried, her mind instantly filling with urgent questions. Was Arvee going to be the one to light the fuse for the crackers? Wouldn't that be extremely dangerous? What about the moisture in the pipes – wouldn't that dampen the gunpowder? How would Arvee get out of the pipes in time to save himself from the blast?

'Ellie, I'm sorry, I've absolutely got to go!' said Arvee. He gave her what he hoped was a brave smile. She had no choice but to give one back to him.

'Take care!' she said.

With a slight jerk, Arvee pushed himself away from the edge of the pipe and went down into it, head first.

21

LIZARD-BACK RIDERS

While Arvee and Ellie were climbing to the roof, Sparx and Willing were getting ready to go lizard-back riding. Two huge old house lizards lay patiently on the sill of the kitchen window as the two young mice struggled to strap themselves securely on to the lizards' backs. The only way to manage this was to lie on their tummies, with their arms looped through strong rubber bands, and the bands looped round the lizards' legs. It was quite a job!

'Well, now,' said the lizard on whose back Sparx was lying, 'don't you mice wish you had sticky pads like we lizards have under our feet? Then you wouldn't need all those straps and buckles to stay attached to us on this little ride.'

Willing muttered in a tone that he expected only Sparx to hear, 'If we had sticky pads, we wouldn't *need* to ride lizard-back.' But before he had finished speaking, his lizard mount chuckled deep in her throat and said, 'Careful what you think, Master Mouse! We lizards are telepathic. We can read your thoughts.'

That shut Willing up completely.

Sparx's mount said, 'Never mind, never mind – let's be off then. Introductions before we start: my name's Ghutghut-Thak A'thet. Thak for short.' She had a very deep voice and spoke in a slow, deliberate fashion. 'And my colleague's name is !Rhick!rhick!chk! Chugh – !Chugh for short.' The second name required a special clicking noise to be made in the lizard's throat, sounding like an exclamation mark.

'So . . . you're on your way to the master bathroom, eh?' said Thak, not waiting for an answer. 'And are we clear about the price? Three Giddy Moths each?'

'Uh, yes, Ma'am,' said Sparx, figuring that it was polite to answer out loud even if Thak could hear his thoughts. 'Three Giddy Moths, but on credit, since we'll have to catch them specially.'

'Good!' she said. 'And I can tell from your thoughts that you're not lying. OK, hold on tight and – please, control your whiskers, if you don't mind. They're tickling the back of my neck.'

The lizards' route was along the outer wall of Paradise Villa. The mice had explained that they must avoid attracting the attention of any rats or rat spies or hungry owls. So Thak and !Chugh made sure that they always moved in the shadows of overhanging ledges or along the grooves between exposed bricks.

Presently they came to the small ventilator in the master bathroom. 'Here we are,' said Thak, 'we'll wait for you outside – oh, wait, that's not what you want?' She paused to concentrate on what Sparx was thinking. 'Ahh – you want us to take you inside. That'll be an extra charge, if you don't mind.'

The ventilator was the kind that has strips of thin glass set into notches in a wooden frame. It was easy for the lizards to wriggle through. The house was built in the old style, with tall rooms and high ceilings. The small window was set up near the ceiling. Once inside the bathroom, Sparx pointed at the tub far below.

'We have to go *there*,' he said to Thak. 'And on to the rim of the tub. But we need to get to the other side, where the taps are.'

The window was set into the wall nearest the foot of the tub. The taps were at the other end.

'Right!' said Thak shortly. 'I do hope you don't mind heights.' And with that she stepped off the wall and on to the ceiling, with Sparx clinging to her back, upside down. It had felt odd enough to be travelling sideways along the walls of the building, but now it was really strange to see the world turned completely upside down. Meanwhile, !Chugh and Willing were following behind, also upside down.

'No, little mouse,' said Thak, in response to Sparx's thoughts, 'we don't have glue on the undersides of our feet, but a very advanced kind of suction pad.' She chuckled deep and low. 'Yes, it *is* a nuisance to have your thoughts read – but just think of the energy you save on not having to talk!'

When they reached the wall close to the tap-end of the tub, both lizards stopped. They were stationed directly above the showerhead. 'As you can see,' said !Chugh, 'there are glazed tiles on the wall just near the head of the tub. Our foot-pads don't work so well on very smooth surfaces so, if you don't mind, we'll set you down on the showerhead.'

The showerhead protruded from the wall just above the place where the glazed tiles began. Thak went first, creeping on to the shaft of the outlet and waiting while Sparx disentangled his arms from the rubber bands to get off her back. Then she returned and !Chugh did the same for Willing.

Leaving both mice standing on the showerhead, the lizards sidled back along the wall and on to the ceiling once more.

'We'll wait for you here,' called Thak. 'When you're ready to leave, just climb up high . . . and think about it very loudly.'

Thanks, thought Sparx. We will.

'Right,' said Willing to Sparx, 'come on, then – let's get out our rappelling gear.'

Both mice tied one end of their sturdy twine ropes on to the shaft of the showerhead. Then, expertly paying out the line, which was looped round them and through a twist of wire shaped like a rappelling hook to give them control, they descended smoothly down, down, down until, 'Here we are!' said Sparx. 'Right on top of the water spout.'

'No, wait,' said Willing. He was tugging at something inside his pocket, getting out a piece of paper. 'I have a diagram that Arvee gave me. It's of this tap. He told me that it was a strange contraption, not the ordinary kind.'

'And it isn't,' said Sparx, looking closely at what they were standing on. 'Most taps have a sort of twiddly thing, which has to be turned. I don't see anything like that here.'

Willing said, looking at the drawing in his hand, 'That's right – there's no twiddly thing. There's only a – a sort of lever thing. Do you see anything that looks like it?' He showed the drawing to Sparx.

There was very little light in the bathroom. Sparx squinted hard, holding the bit of paper this way and that. The two mice were so busy staring at the paper that they didn't notice a slight breeze that came in from the door that connected the bathroom to the bedroom where Mo's parents were fast asleep. Someone had opened that door. Someone had heard sounds from the bathroom. Someone had come inside to investigate. Someone with excellent eyesight and a severe grudge against mice . . .

22
SWEPT AWAY

Meanwhile, back on the roof, Toon and his friends had pulled all the crackers up. Stringer and Ding had also come up and been introduced to the little team gathered there, while Lucky stayed down to keep an eye on Moonie and Gramps.

Toon explained what had to be done. 'Basically, we're consolidating the stuff from inside these little firecrackers to make one really big cracker.' He held up an old sock. 'This is what we'll use to make the new cracker and Feather will show you what else it needs so that it'll go off properly when we light the fuse.'

'Isn't all of this very dangerous?' Ding wanted to know. 'After all, firecrackers use gunpowder and that's what humans use to make bombs.'

'Yes, a firecracker *is* a kind of small bomb,' said Feather. 'But if we're careful and work slowly, nothing will go wrong. The danger is to people – especially young humans – who handle firecrackers without knowing what they're doing. But Arvee has shown us what to do. We're sure there's nothing to be afraid of as long as we follow his instructions carefully.'

'Who'll light the fuse?' asked Stringer, who had been following the various details of the plan closely. 'How will that animal get out from inside the pipes? It seems to me, this scheme hasn't been thought through carefully!'

Toon had to agree that there were some aspects that needed fine-tuning, but, 'We'll have a bit of time once Arvee's blocked the pipe,' he said. 'When he comes back from doing that, he'll have it all worked out – and I'm sure he won't think of anything that'll put us in danger.'

Stringer nodded, but privately he told himself that he wouldn't relax till he knew exactly how the fuse was going to be lit. Fire is a very dangerous thing, to all animals, he thought. Fire and gunpowder combined are . . . he shrugged . . . more dangerous than I want to think about. For all his thoughts, Arvee's only a little mouse in the end. What can he achieve? What can any of us achieve against the powerful forces opposing us?

However, he didn't voice his fears. The team set to work quickly.

Alone at the top of the V-pipe, Ellie watched as Arvee disappeared down into the narrow shaft. She wished she didn't feel so uncertain about the plan. Everyone was working hard but . . . it was also such a big gamble. If, for some reason it, didn't work out, the rats would be mad with fury that the mice had planned a revolt.

She had never doubted Arvee before, but now . . .

She remembered what her father had said when they had first seen Arvee, right in the beginning. How he had warned Ellie that the strange pale mouse would only mean trouble for all of them, that it was best to keep their distance from him. Her whiskers drooped with sadness because she didn't want to believe any of it.

If only she could talk to Arvee now, Ellie thought, he would find some way of calming her anxieties so that, miraculously, everything would seem all right again. She took in a deep breath. What had he said? 'Think slowly and methodically – don't make mistakes.' He was so sure it was wrong for the mice to be terrorized by the rats that he was willing to put his whole mind and energy towards working out a solution to the problem. By contrast, Ellie and her family had given up believing that solutions were possible.

If Arvee could tell her what to do right now, it would be that she should do whatever was best in the situation. That way, even if the plan ended in disaster, at least no one could complain that it was for lack of effort.

With that thought fixed firmly in her mind, Ellie squared her shoulders and sat straighter at her post. Her job, at this moment, was to lower Arvee down slowly on his rope and – to wait. Wait for the signal that he wanted her to stop and then wait for the signal that it was time to haul him back up. So that's what she would do, to the best of her ability. She would not allow destructive thoughts to block her chances of doing the right thing when the time came to do it. She would have faith in the plan and in Arvee's methods.

She looked up at the stars winking far above in the night sky. On a sudden impulse she winked back at them, 'I believe in myself!' she said to the stars. 'Do you?' And she giggled at her own audacity.

Arvee descended slowly towards the bottom of the narrow ventilation shaft. It was a good thing he had greased himself because the pipe was almost too narrow. But the combination of the cream and the balloon-suit made it possible for him to push himself downward.

He could smell the water in the pipe beneath him. He was holding his forearms in such a way that he could easily unfold the balloon he was going to use for blocking the main pipe. Even so, it wasn't going to be an easy task!

In another few minutes, his nose told him that he was just above the water. It was pitch-dark in the pipe, so he had to hope that his nose was correct. He started blowing into the balloon. He pushed it down as he blew, knowing that it must be in the water when it began to expand sideways into the main pipe. As soon as he judged it was big enough, he tied its mouth securely with a bit of string he had brought with him. He also tied a knot in its neck for extra precaution.

Then he began to wrestle with it, to push it into the pipe, in the direction of the water tank. He soon realized that, as long as he was above the balloon, it was going to be a losing battle. There was no option. He was going to have to untie himself from the nylon string, get into the water and shove.

He clanged his paper clip on the side of the pipe to tell Ellie that he was untying himself from the string. A responding signal told him that she had heard and understood. Then he adjusted the plastic bottle cap so that it covered his nose and he undid the knot round his waist.

Wriggling his body, he squeezed his legs round the springy mass of the balloon, keeping to the side leading towards the master bathroom. Very soon his legs were in the water. A sensation of coldness and wetness came through the balloon-suit, but his fur remained dry. Taking a deep breath, and bracing himself against the sharp angle where the V-pipe met the main pipe, Arvee *pushed* . . . and . . . the balloon began to move again, into the right side of the pipe, towards the tank.

Push, shove, push, shove, push, shove . . . thank goodness for the face mask! Arvee's head was soon completely underwater as he struggled with the bulging balloon. But there was enough air inside the plastic bottle cap for him to breathe quite comfortably.

Arvee pushed with his arms, he butted with the front end of the face mask, he shoved with his knees. His muscles screamed with the strain, the air in the face mask was growing moist, he was starting to breathe in short gasps, until finally . . . it was done!

Arvee's head was no longer underwater but sticking up inside the V-pipe once more. The balloon was in place, blocking the main pipe.

He tore off the face mask, gasping for air. How wonderful it was to breathe freely again! The soft, spongy mass of the balloon was just in front of him. Behind him stretched the pipe leading towards the master bathroom. Sparx and Willing were probably there right now, getting ready to open the tap in the tub.

Arvee sat on the plump bulge of the balloon, half in and half out of the water. He pushed his face mask down so that it rested on his tummy, with its elastic tucked out of the way, under his armpits. The nylon string dangled invitingly in front of his nose. I have a moment to catch my breath, he thought, before the boys open the tap.

Two seconds later, however, he realized he was wrong.

23

LOOK OUT!

'There's another thing,' Willing was saying to Sparx. 'Arvee said to be very sure not to turn on the hot water by mistake.'

'Why?' said Sparx. 'What difference does it make?'

'Something about the water coming from the geyser instead of directly from the tank on the roof . . .'

At the door to the bathroom, listening to this exchange, stood the great, dark shape of Alphonso. The fur on his back bristled with excitement.

'I must say,' continued Willing, looking down at the shining metal surface on which they were standing, 'I've never seen a tap like this before. Where's the lever that Arvee says is supposed to be here?'

'Search me!' said Sparx. 'I wish we'd had a little more time to study the mission carefully.'

'Hmmmrrrrr,' purred the big cat softly to himself. 'So the mice are up to something, are they? And in the master bathroom too! Hmmmrrrrrrhhh! How interesting,' he muttered, crouching down, preparing to slink very slowly, very carefully forward, his huge, orange tail swishing from side to side. 'How very, very *interesting*!'

The bathroom was in darkness. The two old lizards, high up on the ceiling, caught no hint of Alphonso's progress.

'There's a lever and we have to pull it up,' said Willing to Sparx. 'But we have to be sure *not* to turn it, or else the water will flow out of the geyser and not the tank . . . and how do we know which way is or isn't the correct one?'

'No clue!' said Sparx, shrugging. 'What did Arvee say? Is it usually the left side for hot water? Or the right? And what are we supposed to turn, anyway?'

Alphonso hadn't forgotten the humiliation of the table-room. He hadn't got over the shame of being confined to the master bedroom ever since. Here was a chance to get even! The voices don't sound like that stuck-up snob of a white mouse, he thought to himself, but some mouse is better than none!

Stealthily, his white belly close to the floor and his claws buried deep inside his big, soft paws so that they would not click against the bathroom tiles, he crept towards the tub.

'Well, look,' said Sparx, 'according to the diagram, we should be able to see this lever from directly overhead. So why don't I go back up the rope and see if I can't spot it from there?'

So saying, with Willing to give him a hand, he climbed back on to the rope.

Alphonso crept closer.

When Sparx was halfway up, he looked down to where Willing was standing. No sign of any lever, except . . . and then, all of a sudden, he understood.

'Willing! How stupid we've been! The lever is the thing we've both been standing on! The spout of the tap is underneath it.'

'Wha – ?' Willing looked down at his paws in surprise. He saw that Sparx was right. He was standing on the lever. Beneath it was the broad spout of the tap. 'Righty-oh! And we've not shifted it either to the right or to the left, so that's OK too. Now – all I need do is tie my end of the rope round the lever, while you continue up.'

The plan was to loop the rope round the lever, then draw it up and over the showerhead and all the way back down. That way, if the mice pulled on the rope the lever should be raised up.

Sparx climbed the rope nimbly. When he was at the showerhead, he heard Willing call out to him, 'OK! The loop's in place. You can loosen the rope and let the whole length of it fall free, over the showerhead. I'll stand here, to make sure the loop doesn't slip off the lever.'

Sparx did as he was told. He weighted the free end of the rope with a fat knot, then he let it down. It was long enough that the end dangled a couple of centimetres lower than the spout of the tap and a few centimetres in front of it. Pulling on the rope a couple of times to make sure it was fastened firmly, he started to clamber down.

Almost immediately, he heard a soft wail from Willing. 'Oh no!' he called to Sparx. 'I've just realized something!'

'What?' asked Sparx.

'Your weight's never going to be enough to pull the lever up!'

'Are you sure?' squeaked Sparx.

'Of course I'm sure – oh, it's all hopeless – we should give up. We're just mice! We can't be expected to turn on water taps. This plan's not going to work after all . . .'

'. . . but not on account of *our* failure!' said Sparx stubbornly. 'Come on – we've got to find a way!' He continued moving down the rope. 'Supposing we both hang on to the end of the rope and swing really hard? Wouldn't that be enough?'

'I don't think so,' said Willing dolefully. 'You're bouncing around quite a bit already and I've not felt the slightest little hint of movement from this lever.'

'I'm not ready to give up,' said Sparx. 'We'll just have to think of something.' He was now almost level with Willing. The end of the rope dangled a centimetre or two beneath him.

All the while, the great, golden cat was moving silently forward. 'Just stay right where you are, little mice, foolish little mice . . .' he whispered in his secret heart, '. . . right . . . where . . . you . . . arrrrrrre . . .' He was at the foot of the tub. Furtively, he raised his head.

'Well,' said Willing, 'you could try to swing towards me. Then I could catch hold of the end of the rope . . .'

He walked out towards the end of the lever. Sparx was level with him and swinging for all he was worth, trying to budge the tap.

The two mice were concentrating so hard that they didn't see Alphonso looking over the rim of the tub. Nor did they see him assessing the distance between the foot of the tub and the spout of the tap, above which they were. 'Slooooowly does it,' said the cat to himself, 'sloooowly . . .' Until now, he'd been under cover of darkness. The moment he hauled himself on to the white rim of the tub, he'd be visible to the mice. But the two little creatures were much too engrossed in their own business to notice him.

Silent as a shadow, he leaped up on to the tub.

'All right!' said Willing. 'Keep swinging, you're almost there . . .'

Suddenly, there was a very loud sound: *'Thk-Thk-Thk-Thk-Thk!* And again: *'Thk-Thk-Thk-Thk-!Chugh!'* It was the lizards, sounding an alarm!

Willing, startled, looked up. 'OOOH!' he screamed to Sparx. 'The cat!'

Alphonso heard the lizards too. He wasted no more time. With his great paws outstretched and his claws fully extended, he launched himself towards the mice.

Sparx registered the lizards' warning, but before he could react, the cat was already airborne – and Willing was shouting.

'This way!' cried his friend. 'On to the lever!'

Sparx jumped for his life towards Willing.

WHAP!

The cat's paw struck the rope where he had last seen Sparx – and snagged the knot at the end of it. THUMP!

The full force of Alphonso's weight bore down on the rope as he landed in the tub.

HUP!

The lever above the spout of the tap sprang up, catapulting Willing and Sparx into the air, like a pair of acrobats.

FOOOOOOOOOOSSSSHHHHHHHHH!

With a breathy roar, the water poured out.

'EEEE-YOWWWWWWWWW!' shrieked Alphonso. 'I *hate* water!'

He shot out of the tub like a rocket. The two mice slammed into the shower curtain. They slid all the way down and thudded on to the tiled floor of the bathroom. Too stunned to move a whisker, they lay helplessly on their backs. Any moment now, they knew, the cat would be upon them.

But Alphonso had no attention to spare on mice. He fled out of the bathroom and under the bed of the Master and Mistress. His luxurious paws and whiskers were soaked through and one of his claws was badly twisted from being caught in the rope. The dust under the bed felt disgustingly mucky on his beautiful fur. But he didn't make a sound. He began to lick himself clean, methodically and thoughtfully. Better to forget all about mice, he told himself. Better to return to the way he was before those rascally rats moved into the house.

I'll study yoga, he thought, I'll become a strict vegetarian, I'll write romantic poetry . . .

24

THE ROACH APPROACH

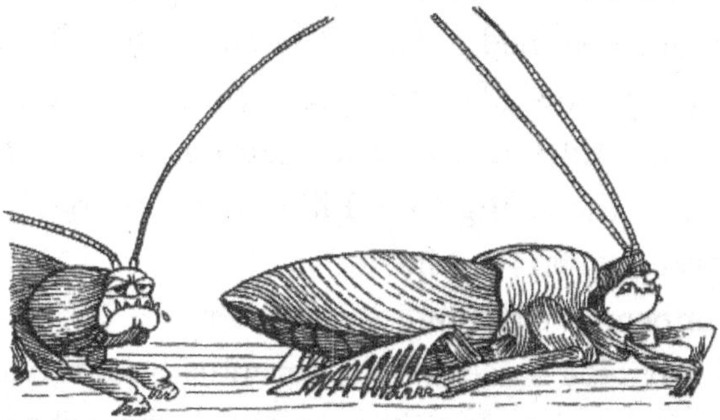

Arvee didn't have time to react. One moment he was sitting on the balloon, half immersed in water, and the next – WHOOSH! – he was gone. The water released by the tap in the master bathroom poured out and down the pipes like a tidal wave. Arvee was sucked away by it before he had time to realize what was happening.

Up at the top of the ventilation pipe, Ellie almost fell off her perch. The force of the rushing water pulled air down the pipe, producing a terrible gurgling, groaning sound that almost deafened her. The slender pipe shook as violently as if a human were kicking it.

'Arveeeeeeee!' screamed Ellie. 'Arveeeeeeee! Where are you!'

But the string in her hand had been slack for some moments before the catastrophe. Arvee had signalled that he was going to untie himself. She had waved back that she understood. After that she had heard nothing more until the horrible noise began.

Without needing to be told, she knew that it was caused by the tap being turned on in the bathroom. She knew that Arvee had nothing to hold on to if he wasn't tied to the string. She knew he must have been swept away by the tide. In fact, she realized, if he *had* been attached to the string, she, Ellie, would probably have been jerked down the pipe too . . .

An unbearable despair gripped her.

The groaning noises stopped eventually and so did the shuddering motion. But Ellie remained where she was. It was like all her worst nightmares coming true together.

She couldn't move or think or feel anything. Everything had failed. Arvee's way of solving problems wasn't foolproof after all. He was the first to acknowledge that all plans were vulnerable to the element of chance. It seemed like chance had taken its toll now.

Far away in the distance she could hear Toon and the others. But Ellie couldn't move her head to look at them. She felt as if she had been turned to stone.

She didn't want to speak to anyone just now. She couldn't bear the idea of doing anything aside from remaining exactly where she was, perhaps forever. She should be telling the others to stop working and to give up. But she didn't have the energy, or the will, to do even that.

Then an odd thing happened.

The thought came into her mind that whatever happened to Arvee, there was no reason for the plan to come to a halt. It was such a clear, simple, obvious thought, almost as if Arvee himself had been sitting by her side, telling her not to give up. That was exactly what he would have said, if he could have been there to say it.

She was sure of it. Sentiment and emotions shouldn't get in the way of doing the right thing, especially if the right thing was something that involved lots of other friends and family. This situation certainly belonged in that category.

So long as Ellie didn't give in to her sadness, thinking that she would never see Arvee again, the plan could just continue in the direction it had taken so far. He had talked about the need for each mouse to be able to fulfil his or her part in the campaign as well as any other mouse. That way, if any one failed, the others could still carry on. Even Arvee's role in lighting the fuse, Ellie realized, could be performed by someone else – *something* else, rather. A bizarre new idea presented itself to her. Perhaps even a better one than its predecessor.

Now Ellie turned round. From where she sat, she could just make out where the rest of the group was.

She felt completely calm. She knew exactly what to do and how to do it.

Soon she was trotting across the roof to where the others were. Toon greeted her. 'Hi, Ellie. We're almost ready. How did Arvee manage?'

'Just fine,' said Ellie. 'He blocked the upper pipe and the water's drained out of the lower pipe.'

'Great!' said Toon, looking relieved, 'I was really worried about the timing.'

'It was perfect,' said Ellie, without turning a whisker. 'And you know what? He had a brainwave about how to fire up the cracker without any one of us being in danger.' Of course it was really her idea, but she didn't tell the others that. She knew they would trust it more if she said Arvee had thought of it. When she described it to the team, everyone cheered.

Two hours later, everything was in place. Zero, Heavy and Horse made sure that the cracker-sock had been lodged securely inside the pipe, just above the Ratland leak. All along the way from the bottom of the ventilation pipe to where the crackers were, the surface had been wiped dry so that the gunpowder wouldn't get damp. Then the fuse was set.

Bits and pieces of the clothes that Arvee had removed while putting on his wetsuit had been strewn inside the pipe right up to the cracker. The largest scraps were stuffed inside one end of the mini-bomb.

They had barely finished their preparations when the first members of the Roach Squad lumbered into view. Up the guttering they came, following Arvee's scent-trail. They walked ponderously, in formation, fourteen gigantic roaches. Ellie, who was hiding close to the ventilation pipe along with most of the team, shuddered inwardly at the sight of the marching insects. They really looked mean!

They came straight across the rooftop to where Feather was sitting innocently, as if it was completely normal for a young mouse to be found out in the open, on the roof, in the middle of the night. The Squad asked no questions. Grabbing her roughly by her arms and her legs, two of the roaches knocked her over on her back while two others twiddled their sensitive feelers carefully across her body. No doubt about it: just the fact that she'd been in Arvee's company a few hours ago was enough to arouse their suspicions.

She could hear the weird, snapping sound made by their ceaselessly clicking sideways jaws as they drooled over her. The stiff hairs up and down their jointed legs poked and scraped her fur. They would have eaten her alive except that they preferred rotting rubbish. And they'd probably been well fed before setting out on their mission or else they'd never have got any work done. The Roach Squad was notoriously easy to bribe: the right food at the right time and they could be distracted from any investigation.

They weren't like living creatures at all, decided Feather. More like machines, which breathed and twitched, with a bit of hunting down, torturing and terrorizing on the side.

When they concluded that Feather wasn't the mouse they were looking for they backed away with that curious floaty-jerky motion they had. No words were exchanged but feelers were twiddled high in the air and there was a sort of scraping, creaking communication. Feather's smell wasn't strong enough for her to be the mouse they were after, not by a long shot. But the animal they were after had been somewhere close by, very close. One after the other, the roaches were turning their small triangular heads and looking over their shoulders in a particular direction.

Feather risked looking around from where she continued to lie on her back. Not far from her, Happy was flitting about apparently unaware of the attention she provoked from the roaches. Would they fall for the bait?

Yes! Slowly, the whole team began to wheel towards her.

Unlike Feather, she didn't remain stationary. Instead, she ran from the roaches, making for the ventilation pipe. In her hand was one of Arvee's sneakers. The insects were very fast and a couple of them were starting to take short, flying leaps. They could fly when they wanted to, but if they took wing, they'd lose sight of the mouse. Happy ran swift as the wind and in a short while had reached the ventilation pipe.

Once there, she clipped the shoe on to the nylon string that Ellie and Arvee had climbed up. In another few seconds, she'd sent the shoe soaring up the pipe, up to the very top, and then she nipped away and out of sight.

The Roach Squad followed right on her heels but when they reached the foot of the pipe, they stopped. They seemed to be confused. The scent-trail they were following had come right up to this point but . . . ? Where had it gone? It was strong, but fading as well, fading fast. They turned their feelers this way and that, opening their senses to the breeze, smelling, tasting and feeling every atom of air.

From the distance of a few metres, Happy and the other mice watched with bated breath. They knew very well that the roaches might prefer the course of chasing after live mice who had Arvee's scent on them rather than after a sneaker. But a white mouse with the right scent was what they were after. They were not skilled at working solutions out for themselves. A white mouse with the right scent was what they would get.

Sure enough, with ponderous precision, each huge insect came to the same conclusion: the source of the smell had gone up the pipe. So they began to climb up . . . up . . . up . . .

At the very top of the pipe, Zero sat with the sneaker dangling at the end of the same nylon rope that Arvee had tied round his waist. The moment the first roach appeared at the top, she dropped the shoe down the shaft of the pipe. The roach hesitated only momentarily, twiddling its feelers in her direction. But Arvee's scent was strong on the nylon rope. The insect teetered delicately at the edge of the pipe and then, curling its surprisingly flexible body over, it tucked its feelers down towards the bottom of the pipe and began to descend. It seemed very particular about remaining close to the string as it went.

Just as the last of its six legs disappeared down the pipe, Zero reached into a pouch she had in her left hand and sprinkled a liberal handful of gunpowder on to the roach's hairy legs. Meanwhile, the next Squad member appeared at the top of the pipe. Each one did exactly what the one before it had done. Each one in turn got a sprinkling of gunpowder. The chunky grains lodged easily on the multijointed limbs of the insects. They seemed not to notice. They were used to being completely covered in sand and grit. This was just more of the same.

When the last roach had appeared and been sprinkled, Zero leaped up and around to the place where the ropes met at the top of the pipe. The nylon strands had been looped together. As an added precaution, Zero wiped the last of the gunpowder from the pouch on to the rope. Then she twinkled down to the roof, where the rest of the group had come out of hiding.

'Right!' said Toon. 'Time to light the lamp! Stand well back, Zero. The rest of us have all had time to wash the gunpowder off ourselves.' He didn't need to warn her twice – she'd already sprinted a safe distance away.

All eyes watched anxiously as Toon's lighter flared. First he held it to the tip of a long dry splinter of bamboo. Instantly, it caught fire. Gingerly, extending his arm as far as he could away from himself, Toon leaned towards the lower edge of the nylon string that dangled outside the ventilation pipe and touched the bamboo splinter to it.

POOM!

All the mice jumped away in fright as, with a snickering hiss, the bright flame shot up the nylon string, up, up, up into the night.

'Back!' called Toon. 'Stand back! Burning bits of string may fall at any moment.' Like a jagged yellow blade, the flame raced to the top of the pipe and, once there, it flared right around the rim . . . seemed to hesitate . . . then dipped its head and went in.

A cheer went up from the mice.

'Wait, wait!' cried Toon. 'Don't let's cheer too soon and in any case we won't see anything.'

'I don't care,' said Feather. 'We've succeeded this far. We did everything we could. It's time to celebrate!'

A plume of white smoke issued from the top of the pipe for a few seconds, then drifted away. Then another. And then a third. It wasn't possible to be sure what was going on inside the pipe, but it seemed fairly clear that the roaches were starting to go up in flames, one by one. A strange, rattling sound from inside the pipe suggested the sound of insect bodies hurtling wildly down within it. They wouldn't have room enough to turn around and come back up. They could only go forward. All exits had been carefully shielded with aluminium foil. The only path they could take was towards the fuse of the cracker bomb.

'They must be running like mad,' said Horse. 'I do think it was a rather horrible thing to do – even to roaches – to use them to light the fuse.'

'Just think of the number of mice they've tortured,' said Toon, darkly, 'and you won't feel sorry for them.'

'I agree with Feather,' said Stringer. 'It's time to celebrate!' His fears had vanished with his admiration for Arvee's inspired scheme.

'Not without Arvee!' said Ding. 'He's the one who should be with us, rejoicing too – where is he, anyway?'

Ellie, who had been standing a little apart, said nothing. She wondered how long it would be before the others understood that, even if everything else went right, at least one thing had gone terribly wrong. But she didn't want to share the sad news with them just then, while they were still feeling so hopeful.

Heavy said, 'He couldn't be with us because of the Roach Squad, right? That's why he had to be away from the roof.'

'Yes – but,' said Happy, 'didn't he say where he'd meet us once the roaches had gone?'

'We still have one more thing to do,' said Ellie, quickly. 'There's the balloon to be punctured yet.' She and Toon had rigged a simple wire device with a sharp nail at the end of it to accomplish this from outside the ventilation pipe.

'How will we know when it's time?' asked Zero, who had joined them again.

As if in answer to her question, a muffled boom sounded from far, far away.

It sounded exactly like thunder but as if it had come from deep inside the house.

'It's the bomb!' cried Toon, jumping up and down excitedly. 'We've won, we've won, we've won!'

Even as he raced towards the ventilation pipe to puncture the balloon and unblock the main pipe, lights in Paradise Villa were being slammed on.

'The humans are waking up,' remarked Ellie. 'They must have heard it too.'

25

A NEW START

Actually, the mice had succeeded beyond their wildest dreams. The rats had tunnelled so recklessly through the foundations of Paradise Villa that Ratland was flooded from end to end when the water was turned on.

It was too much for the old house. The floor beneath Mo's parents' bedroom collapsed. Fortunately for them, they had been awakened by the sound of the explosion. Jumping out of their beds they had run across to Mo's room, fearing some calamity. They were relieved to discover that she was safe but, by that time, since everyone was awake, they decided to have some tea and cookies.

So it was only an hour later, when Mo's parents went back to their bedroom, that they found it in a shambles.

In human terms it was an all-out crisis and needed immediate fixing.

Engineers were called in and the cost of the repair discussed. Precautions for the future were argued over. It was decided that the foundations of Paradise Villa needed extensive renovation. For many months, there would be workmen and machines pounding around the property.

It meant, of course, that all the animals living in Paradise Villa had to move out.

Prior to the flooding, Zero's team had alerted all friendly mice to the possibility of a disaster taking place. Its exact nature couldn't be disclosed, so instead word was put out that an earthquake was expected. The private messenger ants were employed too, to pass information about which areas of Ratland would be the safest to hide in temporarily.

During the flood, many mice took refuge in the unused pipelines which Toon and his friends had been using as alternative routes through Ratland. They were too narrow for the rats, so they provided safe havens till the water receded.

Those mice who chose to remain in Ratland because they couldn't imagine life without the protection of rats, suffered grievously.

The rats were taken completely by surprise. Many lost their lives simply because they couldn't bear to be parted from their luxurious homes and their expensive possessions. Those who survived didn't wait to see what their future prospects in Paradise Villa were. They took what they could with them and vanished from the neighbourhood.

And Pasha? What of him?

His body was never found. Some say he perished in the confusion, clutching his favourite statue, the figure of a pretty slave-mouse. Others say that he saved himself and crept away before his followers could find him and force him to help them to rebuild their lives. Still others say that he lives on, somewhere in Paradise Villa, awaiting his opportunity to get his own back on the mice.

Arvee's friends found him waiting for them in the Stringer family home, to which they returned in triumph soon after hearing the bomb blast. He didn't spoil their celebrations by telling them of his close shave in the water pipe. Privately, though, he praised Ellie very warmly for keeping her wits about her even when she believed she would never see him alive again. It was truly because of her, he said, that the uprising had been such a resounding success.

The plastic bottle cap on his tummy was what saved him. It kept him afloat with his nose above the water as he hurtled along, until he found a joint in the pipe that he could cling to. Once the water stopped flowing into the master bathroom, he cautiously wriggled through the pipes until he found a way to come out near the outlet drain. Sparx and Willing were still in the bathroom, of course, because they needed to turn off the tap before the main pipe was unblocked. They were most astonished to see Arvee, exclaiming over the fact that no one had told them to wait for him. They asked the lizards to call in a third mount, then all three mice were escorted over to the Stringer family home.

Soon after the collapse of Ratland, the Stringers moved into the garden along with everyone else. Their lives had changed so much in the few days just before and just after the flood that the prospect of living in the garden was no longer as terrible as it had once seemed. Moonie and Gramps in particular did well from being in the open air.

Many mice even found themselves wondering why they had waited for the crisis before moving out. As Toon never ceased to say, it was good to smell the earth and to be surrounded by grasses and wild flowers, insects and earthworms and all the other pleasures, ordinary yet wonderful, of nature.

The Stringers dug a comfortable dwelling for themselves just near the row of lantana bushes by the garden wall. In a couple of nights, they had managed to line the whole place with thick plastic waterproofing, with enough space for each mouse to have his or her own room. Other families followed their example. There was space for all.

The weather was warm and pleasant. The mice spent their days sitting in the lower branches of the bushes, swapping gossip, telling jokes and gradually erasing the painful memories of Ratland. Few amongst them remembered the days of glory, when the mice reigned supreme in Paradise Villa. No one missed living in the crowded slums allotted to them by the rats.

Arvee, of course, continued to live in *Mercara* – but he was rarely alone any more. The Stringers were frequent visitors to him and so was he, to their new home. As soon as they had settled down properly, he began teaching Ellie and Toon to read and to write.

He would have liked to have held general literacy classes for all the mice but, as Ellie pointed out to him, that probably wouldn't work too well. After escaping from Ratland, Arvee had scrubbed the hair dye out of his fur. The moment he was white again, the other mice became formal and uneasy in his company.

Though it saddened him, he accepted this as a fact of his existence outside the Laboratory. He didn't try to fight it or force it. Stringer and Toon's team didn't seem to notice and that was enough for him.

One night, almost a fortnight after the Great Flood (as it was now called), he and Ellie were sitting up in the Stringer family bush, enjoying a quiet cup of tea. There was a slight haze in the sky. No stars were visible. But from all around the garden came the small, happy sounds of resettled mouse families adapting to being outside.

'It's really so nice in the garden!' Ellie said. 'And yet – how terrible it had seemed to us when the rats first occupied Paradise Villa.' A firefly, humming sweetly to itself, landed on a leaf right in front her nose. It sat there, blinking, its mysterious brightness lighting up Ellie's face.

She laughed and put a paw out to pat it, but it immediately rose up and flew away, blink-a-blink, blink-a-blink, like a living, flying, neon light. 'How could we ever have thought the outdoors would be bad for us?'

'Well, you know,' Arvee said, 'there's a big difference between being forced to do something and deciding you want to do it.'

Ellie was silent for a moment. Then she said, 'You were forced to leave the Laboratory, weren't you?'

'Yes,' said Arvee. 'Nothing was explained to me and I was sent away with no option to resist, no chance to prepare.' He smoothed back his whiskers. 'I was very unhappy about it at the time. I felt slightly better when I saw *Mercara*, but I wasn't ready to forgive my human colleagues at the Lab. I still felt betrayed by them.'

The firefly had returned, this time with a friend just like itself. The two of them perched unafraid on Arvee's and Ellie's outstretched paws.

'But,' continued Arvee, 'there are some decisions that other people must make for you – because you just don't know enough about the world to make the right choices yourself. Maybe Dr Shah had a very good reason for sending me away and maybe he knew he couldn't tell me about it because,' Arvee shrugged, 'he knew he couldn't have made me believe that I might be happier outside the Lab. Yet I am, now. And his decision was the right one.' He'd never expressed this thought out loud before.

He looked across at Ellie, who appeared to be concentrating very hard on her firefly. It was the kind of moment that would have been perfect for a bit of poetry but, when Arvee opened his mouth, he found that the only words that would come out properly were, 'You know, there's something I still don't understand . . .'

'What's that?'

'Who or what controls the ant line?'

Ellie burst out laughing, 'Oh, Arvee! I'm so glad there are some mysteries left for you to solve!'

To which Arvee replied solemnly, 'Just for that, I'm going to ask you to help me solve another important one.'

'Which is?'

'Who's going to make the next cup of tea?'

'That's easy,' said Ellie. 'Both of us!'

Laughing, they went down to Ellie's house together, followed by the two fireflies.

ACKNOWLEDGEMENTS

Warm thanks to:

Polly Nolan, for her warm and sensitive editing on *Mouse Attack* and for commissioning the sequel *Mouse Invaders*, both first published by Macmillan Children's Books (UK).

Kate Shaw, who agented *Mouse Attack* and *Mouse Invaders*.

Thomas Abraham, for being willing to consider republishing both these titles.

Vatsala Kaul Banerjee, for her warm, firm and always-sensible editorial support, while bringing Arvee and friends to the Indian market in a local edition.

Meena Rajasekaran, for her friendly and patient collaboration, using my drawings in her cover design.